GRAVEDIGGER

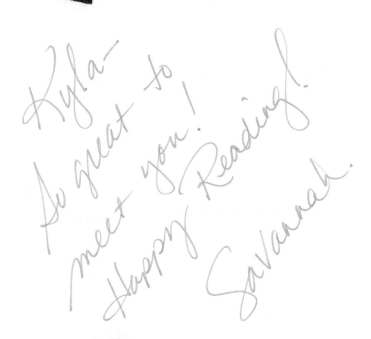

Kyla—
So great to
meet you!
Happy Reading.
Savannah.

Eclectic Bard Books

Gravedigger
By Savannah Verte

Published by
Eclectic Bard Books
USA

Cover design: Funky Book Designs, 2017.
Cover Model: Edward Smith, 2017.

ISBN: 978-1977582508 (Trade Paperback)
AISN: B07527YJ6P (Amazon)

FOR SUZANNA...

I HAVE NO WORDS FOR THIS AMAZING WOMAN. AS MY FRIEND AND MY COVER DESIGNER, SUZANNA HAS GONE ABOVE AND BEYOND ON SO MANY OCCASIONS FOR ME THAT I SHOULD DEDICATE THEM ALL TO HER.

THIS ONE THOUGH...THIS COVER... HANDS DOWN I AM BLOWN OVER AND SO IN LOVE WITH THE WORK. SHE NOT ONLY OFFERED TO TAKE A CUSTOM PHOTO FOR ME FOR THIS COVER, BUT WHEN SHE UNDERSTOOD WHAT I WANTED, SHE LAID IN A GRAVE TO GET THE SHOT.

THAT IS DEDICATION TO CRAFT. THAT IS THE REASON I WILL CONTINUE TO USE HER AND SHARE HER NAME WITH EVERYONE I KNOW. AND THAT IS WHY THIS BOOK IS FOR HER.

THANK YOU SUZANNA. FOR EVERYTHING.

WITH GRATITUDE

To the nameless who inspired me young to remember that everyone has a story, and the one they share isn't always the important one.

To the ones who act to aid without questioning if they should.

To the ones who stop, look, listen, and remember.

May we learn from them, may we encourage them, may we be them.

Lastly, To the ones whose stories are only told in memoriam. May we remember them.

TING...TING...TING...

The soft, rhythmic chiming of the raindrops falling into granddad's old spittoon should have been soothing. Not this time. It was the perfect ending to an imperfect day that left Eric Dublin lost. He was so close. With less than three months to go to retirement, he thought he was going to get to coast the whole way. Not anymore. Instead, the soft ting...ting...ting only reinforced that he was now on a new clock, one that started the moment the body had been found.

Like before, the sound morphed as the brass container filled. Normally, it was only a reminder that the damaged patch of roof above the porch still needed to be fixed.

Today, it shouted that there were other things broken which would, once again, force him to put the repair work off.

For water to be coming in, it meant the wind and rain were coming from the East. This late in the season, when the weather pattern normally brought the problems from the West, it was somehow fitting to have such a distinct change.

Nestled between the Kennesaw River and the mighty Miss, Howard was a one light town with no troubles. A blip on the map that most people missed, it was a short drive from here to anywhere, and most people took the trip. The population fluctuated between three and four digits on any given day, normally well below the four digit threshold when school kicked up in the fall and the students left.

October was typically picturesque with changing leaves and decorated homes. The jovial, simple, pure small town feel had taken a hit less than twenty-four hours before. Now, every ghoul, ghost, and goblin wore a nefarious expression, leaving even the calmest among them, unsettled. Word had traveled fast. The whole town was on edge.

Dublin stared at the raindrops as they streaked the window. He wasn't looking at them, or past them, he was just caught in the absence of thought, trying to make sense of the days' developments. Cal Roundtree, the Corner, wouldn't give his official report for several days, though unofficially he had confided a deep certainty that they were talking about a strangulation. The ligature marks were well-developed, even though it was too soon to officially declare. The autopsy would take place in the morning.

Decades of cases ran through his mind. Dublin honestly couldn't recall the last time Howard had had a homicide. It just didn't happen here. In fact, it was so foreign a notion, that when Gunner Douglas had come racing into the office that morning, Dublin had been sure it was a joke. It took less than a minute to discard the notion as Gunner thrust his cell phone into Dublin's face.

"We've got a fresh one." He had nearly shouted, breathlessly.

"Fresh one what?" Dublin had queried, not quite able to take in the grainy image on the tiny screen.

"Burial. A fresh burial, boss."

"What are you telling me for?" Dublin countered. "Isn't that something you should be telling EJ?"

"No. We didn't do this one." Gunner replied, pacing in front of Dublin's desk. "It's not one of ours."

"What do you mean 'it's not one of ours?'?" Dublin asked as he rose. "How can it not be one of yours?"

Gunner's shoulders came up, as did his hands. "I'd say that's for you to figure out. We just want to know what you want us to do about it."

Dublin crossed his arms across his chest. "So you're telling me you don't know actually what we have. It could just be somebody who buried their dog." He said skeptically.

Gunner stopped mid-step. "It's a mighty big dog then, and I ain't never seen a dog with fingers."

"Define mighty big…" Dublin had started before the comment registered. "Fingers?"

"Well," Gunner paused, his hands moving to measure air, "it's not full-size, but it's better than half. And yeah, fingers."

Dublin forcibly exhaled. "I'll go talk to Hannity and meet you there shortly. Tell EJ to be ready."

Gunner had scooped up his phone and taken off back

the way he'd arrived. If Dublin had any notion of what would come next, he might have better prepared himself. Then again, there's very little that can be done to prepare oneself to unearth the remains of a child. Thinking back, there was only a little consolation in the fact that he wasn't a parent. That small detail might have been the shove needed to push him over the edge.

Thirty minutes later, with Judge Hannity in tow, they'd crossed the yard at the Howard Community Cemetery, to a place near the pond where EJ stood waiting.

"Gunner says it's not one of yours." Dublin opened.

EJ crossed his arms cocking his hip out. "I'm pretty sure I'd know if it was one of mine. Besides, this one is sloppy. And, it's shallow. Nowhere near code or regulation." He replied before hawking a blob of dip-spit off to the side behind him. "'Sides, mine all go in vaults. The fingertips don't stick up through the ground." He finished, head canting to a spot in the middle of the soil patch, wiggling his fingers.

"All right. All right." Dublin answered with his hands up in mock surrender. "It's not one of yours. Any guesses?"

EJ was shaking his head before he spoke. "Nope. Not a one. Fingers aren't large, but ain't small either. I can make out three of them without disturbing anything, each with short, dirty nails. Either chewed on or broken."

Dublin looked at Hannity, whose blank stare was keenly focused on the fingers. "Your call."

Hannity snorked on his inhale. "No call to make here, son. Gotta open her up."

"You heard the man." Dublin nodded to EJ and Gunner. "Open it up."

Hours later, the corpse finally exposed, the four of them stood in disbelief. The boy was a teenager at best. It didn't take a spoken question to answer that none of them had any clue who this child was.

"I'll call Cal." Dublin said to no one in particular.

"Gunner," EJ began. "Go get the tent cart. I'm just spit-balling, but we probably need to be covering this." He said, looking more at Dublin than Gunner as he spoke.

"Good call." Dublin replied. "I'll be back. I need to get some things from the office. For now, nobody says a word about this."

CROWDED

By the time he returned, less than an hour later, there were easily fifty people clamoring around the tent, trying to get a look. Dublin was fuming as he made his approach.

"Y'all get on home now. There ain't nothing here for you to see, and I'm not going to be telling you anything either." He shouted, waving his hands. "I'm sure each of you has got something better to be doing right now. When there's something worth sharing, we will. Go on now, get."

He glared hard at EJ as he ducked under the man's outstretched arm, holding the tent flap open for him to enter.

"Don't look at me." EJ countered the unspoken accusation.

"Gunner?!" Dublin charged.

Gunner put both hands up, one with the mallet for the stake he was driving to stay the tent, the other with the plastic straw he'd pulled from his mouth to respond. "I have not left this spot other than to go get the tent cart. I spoke to no one."

"You can both bet your asses that Hannity hasn't told

anybody, so who does that leave?" Dublin asked.

EJ and Gunner replied in unison. "Nettie Jade."

"Who the hell told her?" Dublin charged, his fingers splayed wide as he dropped his tools in anger.

EJ was tsk-ing, shaking his head, nearly chuckling. "You honestly believe anyone had to tell her anything? Hell, that woman probably knew it was coming before it happened."

"That's really not helpful." Dublin glared. "Seriously, how does she know?"

Gunner rolled his eyes. "Dublin. She works here. A raccoon couldn't pass gas here in the overnight hours without her knowing about it."

"She gives me the creeps." Dublin admitted. "But, get her out here. If she's so all-knowing, maybe she knows who this is."

"I heard that!" Nettie's voice came through the canvas. "And, I ain't all knowing." She added as she cleared the tent flap. "I pay attention. Anybody in a five mile radius who has access to the frequency these two use for their two-way radios knows that there was a fresh grave this morning."

"Beautiful. So what you're saying is everybody knows." Dublin dropped his head.

"Pretty much." Nettie replied. "It ain't like there's much else to do in this town. Folks listen to the scanners."

Dublin's shoulders slumped as his head came up and he looked to the sky he couldn't see through the canopy. "Got any good news?"

Nettie looked between the three men's faces, to the body in the shallow grave, and back to Dublin. "Nope." She paused, holding up a finger. "Correction, I do have a piece of good news. He ain't local."

"Let me rephrase that." Dublin replied with an unamused smile. "Do you have any good news that we don't already know?"

"Oh. Then, no." Nettie replied.

Hours later, Dublin was sporting a splitting headache. The noise from the crowd beyond the canvas was nearly deafening. Cal had retrieved the body and left, but not without difficulty. If Dublin had to guess, half the town was camped out in the cemetery waiting for a glimpse, or word, of what had happened. He had nothing to give them. It was all he could do to stifle his groan when he peaked out through the flap. Front and center, waiting for the scoop, was Vivika Turnbull, the local gossip rag columnist, and as luck would have it, news reporter for Channel 10.

As though God were watching, and took pity, Dublin noticed the skies were dark. A storm was coming. All he needed to do was wait for the rain to drive the crowd to their homes.

He had collected every loose piece of anything the sifter's had revealed. It wasn't much. And, if he was honest with himself, every single bit that he had been able to salvage was probably from the boy, not whomever had put him down.

He finally relaxed when he heard the clap of thunder, and the resulting stampede of the crowd away. They waited fifteen minutes, but not a second more. They didn't need to see it, to feel the charge in the air that meant lightning. They were not safe under the tent. Pulling the flap back, he realized he wasn't safe beyond it either. Vivika pounced before so much as a drop of rain could reach him.

"Officer Dublin, what can you tell us? Who was found? Do we have an identification? The rumor is that it's a child, can you confirm?" She berated him with question upon question. One of two left, she and her cameraman were both under umbrellas waiting. The rest of the crowd had dissipated.

"I've got nothing for you Vivika." He answered, changing trajectory to walk around her to the waiting cruiser.

"But, you're not denying anything either, is that correct?" She challenged.

Dublin's shoulders fell and his eyes rolled up as his breath left in a single huff. He quickly counted to ten before turning to respond to her. "I am not confirming, or denying, anything. No story. No comment." He replied succinctly, continuing his three-hundred-sixty degree turn in one fluid movement, walking off before she could get another question in.

RESULTS

Cal had called late to deliver his initial assessment. He'd have more conclusive results after the autopsy, but he was already willing to rule the death unnatural. For the first time in decades, Howard had a homicide.

The six o'clock newscast only upped the ante. Vivika, having not a single fact to report, managed to sensationalize the story, and incite panic. Dublin's phone hadn't stopped ringing since her segment began. Sadly, the only call he wanted, was one he would not get until tomorrow. Cal was unwilling to speculate further.

Dublin was up and at the office early. He had only basic information to go off of, but he deemed that starting his search sooner than later was warranted. The Missing Children's Database only served to provide a new dark cloud. There were hundreds, if not thousands, of missing boys between the ages of nine and fifteen. He was going to need more information to narrow down the possibilities. It was sobering, and he hadn't had a drink in years.

The clock on the wall had barely struck eight before Vivika came soldiering through with her cameraman.

"Officer Dublin, any update? Any comments today?" She challenged with a wide grin.

"Shut that damn thing off, Viv. This isn't a story until I say it's a story, and right now, it isn't a story. Got it?" He charged.

He was surprised when she turned to her accompaniment. "Take five, Max." She said, head canting toward the door. Once they were alone, she leveled him with a hard stare. "You know you can't bury this? Sorry, bad choice of words." She interjected. "This isn't going away. You are going to have to deal with it." She said softly.

Dublin's eyes flew wide. "I am well aware what my responsibilities here are. Thanks for the update though. If that's all you came for, you can follow your cameraman out the door. I have nothing to say to you right now. When we know something, we will do as we have always done, and release the information. At this time, I am not willing to release speculation so that you can add it to your Pulitzer Prize seeking resume." He said, pointing to the door.

To her credit, she almost managed to look hurt. "I am a serious journalist. People have a right to know."

"No. People have a right to know the truth, when the truth is known." Dublin countered, rising from his seat as she lowered into the one opposite him. "People have a right to be protected. People have a right not to be afraid in their homes by the unknown. People have a right to be treated with respect, and dignity, and all the due deference we can offer. That includes after they are no longer alive. Show some respect." He finished commandingly.

"I didn't mean..." She stammered.

"You didn't anything!" Dublin growled, leaning across his desk. "You didn't think. You didn't pause. You didn't bother for one moment, to consider anyone, or anything, beyond yourself. That...is why I have no information for you. And that...is why, if you don't watch your step going forward, you will not be who breaks the story." He snapped his teeth together as he finished.

Vivika's jaw dropped open, the full realization of his words hitting hard. "You wouldn't..."

"I absolutely would."

Dublin listened to the secondhand tick on the wall clock for what must have been a full minute as she stared at him, obviously assessing the veracity of his threat. He recognized the moment she understood the full implications of his words. "You win." She said quietly.

"No." He shook his head. "Nobody wins here. That's the point."

Through the glass partition, Dublin noticed when Tiffany Trace, his secretary, walked in about fifteen minutes late, as per usual. As if on cue, the dedicated line to the coroner's office lit. Unwilling to have a conversation with Cal in front of Vivika, he punched the intercom, stifling a chuckle when Tiffany jumped. "Trace! Please show Miss. Turnbull to the door for me. I have a call." He boomed through the intercom, making eye contact with Tiffany through the glass.

Once he was alone, he snagged the handset, barking into the receiver. "Dublin."

"Good morning to you too." Cal chuckled into the phone. "You probably want to come over for this one. I can give you the basics, but I do have details you're going to want to watch for."

Dublin had no guesses what Cal meant, but if it was something that could help, he'd take whatever he could get. "I'm on my way."

NOTCHES

Dublin hated the antiseptic smell of the morgue. Not quite as much as he hated the smell of decomp, but it was a close second. In many ways, the morgue was sensory overload to his finer sensibilities. The antiseptic smell was just the frosting. Something about the impersonal grayscale tile that butted up to the stainless steel row of doors to drawers that had remained empty for most of his tenure, left him unsettled to see.

He clenched his gut before pushing through to the small room where Cal was working. "Okay. I'm here. What do we know?" He opened, hoping to expedite the visit.

"You want the grocery list? Or, the play-by-play?" Cal asked in a neutral tone.

"However you want to give it to me." Dublin countered, knowing Cal would do it his way regardless of how he answered.

"Lividity is going to fix time of death between thirty-two and thirty-four hours ago. Best guess, between eleven pm Monday night and one am yesterday morning." He opened.

Dublin flipped to a fresh page in his notebook and began

scribbling. Once he looked up again, Cal continued.

"I'd focus your search on boys between twelve and thirteen years old. Cause of death is definitely strangulation. I'll get to that in a moment, it may be helpful." He paused when Dublin held up a finger, making notes.

"Got it." Dublin said, as he dropped his hand back down.

"At first I thought hanging, but the marks are wrong. If you look here," he pulled back the drape to reveal the boy from the shoulders up. "I would guess it was a belt, based on the pattern of pressure marks. These raised double marks fall at a distinct one inch intervals, like notches on the open end of a belt, which is notably odd.

Normally, you would guess the belt would have been threaded through the buckle for force, but I don't see any indication of a buckle. So, either it is the loose end, or the belt is notched all the way through, which is honestly what I am leaning towards, because none of these have pull indications of use. That, or it was brand-new." Cal summarized, scratching his head as he talked through the findings.

"The buckle isn't on the back of the neck?" Dublin queried.

"No, that's what's interesting. It's almost like the two sides were brought together and a different pressure was used to hold it closed." He said, lifting the head, and turning it so Dublin could see. "See how these notches distort?"

"Yes. You know what I'm going to ask you for, right? Dublin baited.

"Already on it. The mold is drying."

"Is it distinct enough that we could use it?"

"I'm hopeful that there will be something about it that we can use to match any we find." Cal offered. "I have no idea if it's common or not."

"Let's hope." Dublin countered. "Anything else?"

Cal shrugged. "I'll have more, and know more once I'm done, but I thought the notches were important. Other things to be aware of, if only for sanity, there was enough ketamine in his system, I don't think he felt it, so there's that. Unfortunately, the same can't be said for other abuses. I think you're looking for a sexual predator."

"Of kids? In Howard? You've got to be kidding me." Dublin voiced his disbelief before he could filter it.

"Yes, of kids. In Howard? I can't say. This boy is not from Howard. And no, I'm not kidding you."

Dublin shook his head. "Remind me to thank you for giving me this information before I had a chance to have breakfast. I think I might be sick."

"I wish I had better news." Cal offered, drawing the sheet back over the child's head.

"Me too." Dublin agreed. "Let me know when the mold is ready, hopefully it helps. I need to go narrow my search and pray for a break. This might be helpful if we have a suspect, but right now I'm empty."

DRY SPELL

The investigation was basically in limbo. Days later, Dublin was no closer to having a suspect, than he was to identifying the boy. The once friendly town had become a near wasteland. Essie's ice cream parlor, while normally slower at this time of year, was empty, save for Essie. After school, children were shuttled home and locked behind doors. There was little street noise, the drug store was empty, and piles of fallen leaves lay waiting to be jumped in. With the absence of anything known, everything unknown became feared.

"So what happens now?" Gunner asked EJ as he kicked his boots up onto the desk and sipped his coffee. "We just wait?"

EJ tipped his head and stared at his assistant. "What would you have anybody do? They don't know who the kid is. They don't know where he came from. They don't know how he got here. Basically, they don't know much."

Gunner scratched his head. "Why are you asking me? I don't know. I'm not the thinker. I just... It's just wrong. That boy needs to be put to rest, not laying in some silver drawer somewhere waiting for what may never come."

"I'm sure there's a rule somewhere about how they do

what they do, and when they can do it. But, if you got some idea on how to make it go faster, I'm sure Dublin would love to hear from you." EJ said with a smirk. "Now, get your feet off the desk, wipe that mud off my calendar, and get your crap, we got a job to do. All the vases need to be turned down before the first."

Gunner scoffed. "You know half of them are going to be turned back up long before we get to Thanksgiving. Why don't we just wait?"

"Because the rules say we turn them down by November first. Anybody that wants to turn theirs back up after, have it get full of water, freeze, break, and then not be smart enough to keep their yap shut about it, can deal with Nettie Jade. Our job is to turn them all down by November first. Cappiece?"

"Yeah, I got you. You, and your Italian." Gunner grumbled.

Dublin looked up as EJ walked in. The groundskeeper didn't speak, only laid a silver identification bracelet on the desk and turned to leave.

"What's this?"

"It's an ID bracelet. We found it while turning vases. I checked all the interment records, we don't have a Kevin Davis. It looks like it's for a child. And, it wasn't too far from where the body was found last week. Maybe it helps." The groundsman shrugged. "I'm not aware of any Davis family in Howard either these days. I thought maybe you could figure it out."

"You think it belongs to the kid?" Dublin queried, raising a single eyebrow.

"Not my department, boss. I know it doesn't belong at the cemetery." EJ countered blankly.

"Thanks." Dublin nodded. "I'll check it out."

FRESH CORPSE

Gunner Douglas was waiting in the drive when Dublin emerged to go to work. What started out to be a perfectly good, normal day, changed dramatically with a single exchange.

"We've got another one." Gunner announced, sounding defeated.

"Qualify that." Dublin countered, his fists clenched. His heart was already racing, hoping that he was misunderstanding, even as he was sure he wasn't.

"We have another fresh grave."

Dublin swallowed hard. "Is it another child?"

Gunner shook his head. "I can't answer that. We haven't disturbed it. It looks to be bigger than the last one though."

Dublin pulled his hand down his face before shoving it back up and through his hair. They'd gotten next to nowhere with the first one. Now, there were two. "Who else knows?"

"Me. You. EJ. And, I would imagine Nettie Jade. No one else has been notified, and EJ and me stayed off the radio about this one." Gunner added with a slight shrug. "We figured that might help keep the crowd down."

Dublin pulled out his cell phone, hitting the speed dial for Judge Hannity. He looked up to Gunner while he waited for the call to connect. "I'll be right behind you."

EJ and Gunner were standing near a rough mound of freshly turned soil when Dublin arrived. The tent cart had already been pulled around, and a pile of tools were on the ground nearby.

"You might as well put up the tent while we wait for the judge. We can't do anything else until he gives us the go-ahead, though I have appraised him of what you told me." Dublin advised.

Leaving the canopy off, the four corners had just been erected, and the drape about to be placed when the judge rolled up. EJ and Gunner stopped to wait as Dublin walked over to the judge's car.

"Any guesses?" Gunner asked EJ without turning.

"Not my department." EJ replied, watching the other two men approach.

Judge Hannity walked a circle around the mound before coming to a stop near the two groundsman. "Same as before?" He asked without elaborating.

"Near as we can tell." EJ answered with a shrug. "Gunner found it morning when we arrived."

Hannity shook his head and turned to Dublin. "Got a nip this. Nip it right in the bud before it blooms."

Dublin scoffed. "Nip it? Nip it is kind compared to what

I want to do. I want to gouge this sucker out by the roots and bleach the soil so nothing else can grow."

Hannity snickered. His hand came up to knead the muscles at the back of his neck. "See that you do that, exactly that. Meanwhile, open this up." He finished, backing away to stand and watch.

Working with hand spades and fat paintbrushes, EJ and Gunner excavated the soil, layer by layer, to expose the fresh corpse. Like the first, the body was not enclosed in an appropriate burial vault. This one however, was deeper than the first. They were nearly a foot down before they uncovered anything. If they had started at the foot end, they would have hit the tips of the shoes sooner, but from the head end, they had to go deeper.

As the face was uncovered, Gunner jumped back and scrambled to get out of the grave. "I know him."

Dublin and Hannity came over to the edge, glancing down. Dublin's eyes went wide. "I know him too."

"Well I don't know him." Hannity said. "Who is it?"

"That's Mr. Culleroy." Gunner exclaimed with a full body shudder. "He lives out on old 43, up the road from where my grandparent's house was. He gave me the willies when I was a kid."

EJ chuckled and wiped his eyes. "When you were a kid? Seems to me like he still does. Or, are you still a kid?"

"Laugh all you want, EJ." Gunner countered, brushing his palms up and down his arms. "He was a creepy dude. Gran told me to steer clear of him. I did."

"How old are you Gunner?" Dublin asked. "I mean, how long ago was this?"

Gunner shook his head. "I steered clear of that crazy

bat," he said pointing, "until the day we sold the property out there. I haven't been there in," he wiggled his fingers as he mouth-counted to himself, "five or six years."

"So, you were never out to his actual property." Dublin asked without asking.

Gunner put both hands up in front of his body. "No way. Not since I was like, ten. Don't get me wrong, he wasn't mean or anything like that. Actually, he was nice, but in a way that made the hair on the back of your neck stand up."

Hannity's eyebrows raised as he turned toward Dublin. "And you said you know this guy too?"

"I know of him, yes." Dublin nodded. "We did a welfare check out there a year or two ago. Started as a report of an unattended fire out of control. When we got there, it was nothing but a big ash pile."

Hannity took off his glasses and pinched the bridge of his nose. He spoke only after he replaced his glasses and focused on Dublin. "I'd say it's high time you do another welfare check out of that property."

"I think you're right."

"But later. Finish this up and get Cal to do his thing. I want to know what happened to Mr. Culleroy. Stop by my office after this is done, I'll have a warrant ready for the property." Hannity concluded before returning to his car and heading off.

Once he was gone, Dublin turned back to Gunner. "You say he gave you the willies, huh?"

"Let's just say I didn't need Gran to tell me twice to leave him be. He made my skin crawl, and my stomach turn. I wanted nothing to do with him."

"How about now?" Dublin asked directly, glancing into the grave that still needed to be excavated.

"I'm not sure I have a choice." Gunner countered, groaning. "Unless…" He glanced hopefully to EJ. "You want to finish this?"

A wicked grin crossed EJ's face. "How much is it worth to you?"

"Probably a lot. What's your price?"

"How attached are you to those game tickets for the Blues against the Blackhawks?" EJ dropped casually.

"That's low man. Bargaining with a man's hockey tickets? Way low." Gunner replied, grinding the straw between his teeth.

EJ sat on the lip of the grave staring Gunner down hard. "See, it's like this, in this hand…" He raised his right hand, complete with the wide angled paintbrush, "I have this thing that helps me do the job here," he pointed into the grave, "that we could do together faster. But, in this hand…" He raised his empty left hand, "I could have nothing, or I could have another tool and hockey tickets. What'll it be?"

"You know if you make me give you my hockey tickets I'm going to hate you, right?" Gunner offered, doing his best not to sound petulant.

"Yes. But, you need to understand I can live with that." EJ answered matter-of-factly.

Gunner whipped the mangled straw from his lips and dropped it, pulling a fresh one from his pocket, tearing off the paper sleeve from McDonald's. "This is robbery. Highway robbery." He pointed with it before jamming it between his teeth.

EJ snorted, fanning the bristles of the paintbrush

between his fingers. "No. It's opportunity. For me, tickets to see the Blues. For you, to get out of doing something you really don't want to do. Maybe that makes it compromise." EJ grinned.

"Fine!" Gunner acquiesced. "Will you at least take me to the game?"

"I'll think about it."

"Harsh EJ. Harsh." Gunner groaned.

Handing over his tools, Gunner finished setting the tent, raising the sides before taking off. He knew he would not get out of that responsibility too. He made it all of five steps, almost clearing the tent, before EJ called him back.

"You ain't done here. Pick up that nasty, knotted straw you threw on the ground. I've already got a pocket full of them from you and your litter bug ways."

Gunner grumbled the whole way, but retrieved his trash, and made his exit. The only good thing that happened was that he didn't have to deal with Marco Culleroy. He already knew he would be scheming for a way to get his tickets back from EJ. But, not today.

Dublin watched the exchange in disbelief, actively trying not to laugh as it played out. EJ didn't pull punches. He's remember.

REVELATION

EJ was careful, but quick. As he watched, Culleroy's body was revealed bit by bit. His heart lurched when the man's trousers came into view. Dublin's eyes nearly bugged out of their sockets. Neatly threaded through the loops, was a belt and buckle. The long strip of leather that encircled the man had regularly spaced holes punched in it, two high, roughly an inch apart. He wasn't a numbers guy, but he was more than willing to bet the odds were slim.

"I'll be a son of a gun." Dublin hissed out.

EJ looked up. "What?" He asked, following Dublin's gaze not seeing anything unusual. "What's got you so impressed?"

Dublin pointed. "His belt. I think I've seen it before."

EJ's face squirreled up in confusion. "Okay. Not impressive. It's a belt."

"Maybe."

Cal Roundtree came through the flap about that. "You rang?"

Dublin pointed to where EJ continued to work. "Yes.

We've got another one. As soon as EJ gets done, he's all yours. Normal battery."

"I think I can handle it." Cal replied with a chuckle.

Dublin finger called him to step closer, whispering. "I'm not telling you how to do your job, but I need you to check the belt."

Cal stepped over to the edge of the grave and looked down. "Do you think?"

"I think it's peculiar as hell, that's what I think." Dublin countered.

"I'll check it out." Cal said nodding. Turning to EJ, "How much more time do you think you need?"

EJ belatedly caught that Cal was talking to him. "What?"

"How long?"

EJ double checked his progress. Unless there was something below the man that he could not see, they should have little difficulty lifting him up and out. "If you want to get the cart over here, and help me lift them out, we can probably pull him now."

"Works for me." Cal countered. He turned back a moment later. "Why are you working alone? What happened to Gunner?"

Dublin broke into peals of laughter. "Hockey tickets."

Cal's jaw dropped open. "You got Gunner to part with tickets to the Blues?"

EJ grinned. "Leverage is everything."

"You are a savage." Cal remarked, sounding impressed. "Remind me never to bet against you."

With the body back at the morgue, Cal delayed his initial assessment in lieu of pulling the belt to check it against the boy. After carefully extracting it from the loops, he brushed any lingering debris from it, dusting over the individual holes with a vacuum for any particulates they might need to check later. With baited breath, he laid the leather against the soft mold that had been taken from the boy's throat.

"Holy Hannah." He exclaimed when it matched up perfectly.

Regaining his composure, Cal carefully laid the belt out to do a section by section inspection of the leather, the holes, and the buckle under the microscope. Two thirds of the way done, he found the piece that changed the scenario from coincidental to certain. Epithelial cells were mashed into the underside of the leather, and bent over the lip of two sets of the buckle holes.

All total, there were maybe a dozen cells. It was a fractional sample if ever he'd seen one. Still, propriety only allowed him to test half. Preparing them carefully, he let the computer do what he was too shaky to confidently do by hand. He could hardly breathe, and was sure his heart had stopped beating waiting for the results.

When the computer kicked out a positive match for the cells from the belt to those of the boy, he nearly passed out. They still didn't know who the boy was, but they at least knew now who had likely killed him. The problem was, who had killed the killer?

Cal nearly tripped over his own feet trying to get to his cell phone. Dialing Dublin, he forced himself to take several deep breaths and calm down to deliver the news as it rang. When the call connected, he needed to take another before he could begin. "I've got good news. And I've got not good news."

"Uhhhh." Dublin stuttered out, obviously caught off guard. "I suppose that's better than you've got good news, and you've got bad news. What's the not good news?"

"I still have no idea who the boy is." Cal offered.

"And the good news?" Dublin prodded.

"I'm pretty sure I know who killed him."

MIASMA

From 43, the Culleroy property looked like any other farm. If it grew anything other than weeds though, was debatable. The white, clapboard house stood back from the road. Curiously, many of the lights were on. Dublin sat behind the wheel as he pulled the cruiser to a stop, putting it in park.

"Tiffany, I'm 10-23." He radioed in his arrival.

"10-4."

"Standby on this channel. I'm going in."

Walking the perimeter, he noticed no movement inside. Outside, was another story. There had definitely been multiple persons in the area, judging by at least two distinct sets of footprints. He'd have Bud come out and take casts. He wasn't extremely hopeful there would be any matches, but one could never tell.

A chill raced his spine as he came around the back and noticed the porch door was ajar. "Dammit." He said to himself. Pulling out a pair of latex gloves, he covered his hands.

He eased the door open, careful not to touch the handle. Nothing could have prepared him for what he found inside.

The kitchen was all stainless steel, appliances, counters, and nearly every surface. Even the chairs at the table were sterile, and uncomfortable looking. A quick glance across the surfaces left him to believe there would be no prints found.

Through the swinging butler's door was a different story. The parlor was filled with more cameras, lighting, and other equipment he couldn't identify, than probably was needed for a Hollywood set. The chill that had raced his spine and settled between his shoulder blades, made a break down his arms, leaving a trail of gooseflesh in its wake.

A small room off to the side was filled with computer equipment. There were easily enough workstations for three or four people he noted as he glanced in. "What in the world were you up to Marco?" Dublin asked the empty room.

The balance of the rooms on the main floor were empty, eerily empty. The stairs to the second level too, were bare. Dublin noted that there was not a single photograph, knickknack, or personal item on any wall, or any shelf space he could see.

The upstairs bathroom was, like the kitchen, stainless steel, or shiny surfaces. Only the roll of toilet tissue, and the clear shower liner, stood out in contrast. The linen cupboard had exactly 4 towels, four washcloths, two an opened bars of soap, and a small toiletry bag with a razor, a toothbrush, toothpaste, and shaving cream. Dublin was stunned, but not surprised, when the medicine cabinet was also empty.

The next room he entered, likely would have been a bedroom, if there had been anything in it. It was empty. The last room, the master bedroom, judging by the size, was sparse. A double bed and nightstand, a dresser, and a small chair near the window were the only occupants. Like the rest of the house, there was nothing hanging on the walls. Even the windows were only covered with a single roll shade. There were no curtains. In fact, a single comb resting on top of the dresser, stood out dramatically as being out of place.

The dresser held T-shirts, underwear, and socks, but barely enough for a week. The closet too, had few inhabitants. One pair of work boots, a pair of slippers, and several pair of slacks which hung in precise rows, side-by-side with coordinated shirts. The word frugal did not encompass what he was seeing.

Back on the main floor, he encountered several closets before he located door to the basement stairs. For the sterile, cold feel of the rest of the house, the wall of scents that accosted him when he opened this door nearly leveled him. The air here was thick with perspiration, and a miasma of other offensive smells. Dublin stepped back to allow it to vent a moment before he deigned to descend.

Each step down became more excruciating than the last. He was thankful that he was not detecting the smell of decomp, but what he was getting was somehow worse. In his entire career to now, he would've bet big money that there was nothing worse than decomposing human flesh. He would have to reevaluate that.

Reaching the bottom, his stomach lurched at what he saw. The space was cleanly divided into two distinct areas. One side was a wall of three cells smaller than what he had at the jail, each furnished with what he could only estimate was half of a single mattress. The only other contents were a few crude toys. Dublin choked on bile, fighting for it to be nothing more.

The other side was equally disturbing, if not more so.

More stainless steel was outfitted with a mad conflagration of bondage equipment, the likes of which he could not have claimed to have ever seen before, even on pay-per-view. The implications were clear. The urge to vomit became an incessant, immediate imperative. All he had on him was a small evidence bag. He was doubtful that was going to hold it.

Clapping one hand across his mouth, using his thumb and forefinger to pinch his nose closed, he made a run for the stairs, hoping he could navigate quickly and get outside before the inevitable happened. It was close.

His stomach heaved again when the smell of his re-experienced breakfast splashed down and recoiled back. Once he was sure his stomach was empty, he radioed in.

"Tiffany, I'm 10... Screw it. I don't have a code for this. Send Bud out with the van, and a couple cases of garbage bags. I don't think we have evidence bags big enough for this. Then, put in a call to St. Louis. We're going to need a full team." He managed on a groan.

"10-4. Are you okay? You don't sound so good." Tiffany questioned succinctly.

Dublin debated professional versus truth. He opted for truth. "In almost thirty years, I've never seen anything like this. No, I'm not okay. No one would be."

"Copy that, wait for Bud to get there then. Anything else?"

Dublin cringed. It was the last thing he wanted to do, but he knew he was out of his depth. "Call Gray."

"You're sure?"

"No. I'm not sure. Just do it before I have a chance to think about it." Dublin demanded. "That's all. Out."

Dublin dropped into his chair, thankful for a moment the day was ending. The team from St. Louis was taking point on the basement, which suited him just fine. If he never had to go down those stairs again, he wouldn't mind a bit. Bud had managed to cast both sets of footprints outside the home, and they had taken the equipment from the sitting room, or apparent office. They'd pulled the cords & just taken the components. They didn't waste time trying to untangle the wires. The computers would become the focus of his department's attention. His department, and one edgy, spitfire, named Darian Gray.

ONE DOWN

Cal called before coffee. Dublin didn't ask. If Cal was summoning him this early in the day, it was either really good news, or really not. He decided he would wait to hear one way or the other.

There was a cart outside the door with protective equipment and a mask. Dublin groaned. Definitely not good news if he needed this. Fully outfitted, he pushed the door with his elbow, and crossed the threshold. "You rang?"

"I did. I've got answers for you, but not necessarily the ones you want." Cal said.

Dublin would guess Cal was smiling by the way his eyes crinkled, since he couldn't see his mouth for the mask. "Okay, tell me."

"Easier if I show you. I know you love this part." Cal teased.

"Love? Is that what we call it now?" Dublin countered. "Just get on with it."

He clenched his fists as Cal pulled back the sheet to reveal the first victim. Even so close to retirement, he had never gotten used to seeing a body this way. He tried to take several deep breaths in, failing miserably. "Tell me you have nasal paste nearby." He lamented.

"Of course." Cal replied, pointing to the shelf behind Dublin near the door. "Help yourself."

The crisp mint of the nasal paste diminished the smells from the body, and thankfully, the antiseptic too. It wasn't half bad for helping to calm his rolling stomach either, Dublin thought. "Ready when you are."

"So, we've already ascertained the belt is a match for the ligature marks that were left around the throat. The lack of indication for the buckle can be attributed to the double prong style that was used." Cal began.

"Okay. We already sort of guessed that part." Dublin challenged, keeping himself a few steps back from the body.

"Yes. We did. I didn't know definitively though until I had a chance to look at the hyoid. For a child this age, it is usually firm enough, that it would snap in a hanging. This one didn't. There is evidence of stress, though not sufficient to break it. That, coupled with the brain swelling," Cal moved toward the head.

"Stop!" Dublin interjected. "You don't have to show me. Just tell me."

Cal returned to his original position on the far side of the body. "Okay. Basically, the boy was suffocated, or in this case, denied oxygen long enough to result in organ failure, and brain swelling. Cause of death is asphyxiation."

"And?" Dublin prodded, thinking this couldn't possibly be all there was to prompt an early morning call.

"And, I have been able to match residual epithelial cells from Marco Culleroy to other places on the boy's body. Do you want me to show you?"

Dublin debated, staring at Cal. "Do I?"

"Knowing you, probably not." Cal answered. "But, I can. I can also show you where other latent bruises match near perfectly to Culleroy's hands."

"Nope." Dublin shook his head. "I'm good. If you say it's so, I'll take your word for it. I don't want to see that."

"That works." Cal nodded, replacing the sheet over the boy. "I am comfortable declaring homicide by asphyxiation, and Marco Culleroy as the assailant responsible."

"Well that's one." Dublin lamented, pacing to the foot of the steel table and back. "But, he's dead too. Unless you're going to tell me that he took his own life out of guilt or something, we still have a problem."

Cal held up a single finger before rolling the draped table off to the side. Re-crossing his steps, he pulled the lever on one of the small square doors, swung it wide, and extracted a long tray. Pulling back the sheet, Marco Culleroy was revealed to mid-chest. "I have a start on that."

"Did he suffer?" Dublin asked before he could filter.

Cal's head jerked up at the question. "It's distinctly possible."

"I'm sorry. I shouldn't have asked that. I was out at the house yesterday, and somehow the part of me that isn't the Sheriff nudged out the professional just now after what I saw."

"You want to explain that?" Cal asked.

"Not really. When we know more, and definitively, if what I believe is actually true, then yes, you will need to know. For right now, I don't think I can talk through it." Dublin answered, fighting to hold his nonexistent breakfast down.

"Good enough." Cal nodded as he turned the head. "If you look here, you see these small, round bruises? At the very center of them, is a tiny puncture hole. Near as I can tell, it's about the size of an insulin needle. I've been through the medical records. Marco Culleroy wasn't diabetic."

"But I thought most people's bodies produce insulin anyway? Isn't that correct? So what if he got an insulin injection?" Dublin asked. "I don't follow."

"Well…" Cal nodded and bounced his head left to right. "That's true, but at the same time, just like a diabetic person needs regulated doses of insulin, a nondiabetic person doesn't need too much extra. There are consequences either way."

"So, how would you know? Did he get insulin? Did he get too much?"

"As I didn't find anything else in the blood results that was off, an overdose of insulin could be a possibility. If a reasonably healthy person were to get a large dose of insulin, it could send them the other direction, which is hypoglycemia."

"I've heard of that." Dublin chimed in. "We keep stuff in our kits for if we encounter that. The person has to have normal food too, but initially they need sweets to avoid the shakes, sweats, and I think seizures, if I remember correctly."

"Exactly! Those are some of the reactions. Confusion, weakness, and nausea are also on the list of initial symptoms. But, if untreated, it can eventually lead to unconsciousness, or even death." Cal summarized.

"You're telling me he died from an insulin overdose?" Dublin asked in disbelief.

"No. I'm not." Cal leveled.

"Then what? Because it sounds like that's what you're saying."

"I think…" Cal held his hand up, "I think it is distinctly possible that an insulin overdose was used to incapacitate him."

"But not kill him?"

"No. I'm afraid Mr. Culleroy was very much alive when he was buried."

Dublin's jaw dropped open. He popped both index fingers up for Cal to pause so he could process what he had just been told. "You're sure?" Dublin finally managed to voice his astonishment.

"Judging by the soil up his nose, and down his windpipe, I'm nearly positive he took a breath. I'll have a better guess as to how many once I get to the lungs."

"So…?" Dublin prodded.

"He also died of asphyxiation."

Dublin remembered almost a second too late that he had nasal paste on his gloves, pulling his hands back from running his fingers through his hair just in time. "I'll be a son of a gun."

NEMESIS

The roar from his belly announced loudly that it was getting close to lunchtime. Dublin hadn't moved in likely the last hour, mentally processing the information Cal had shared earlier that morning. He absently heard the front door open, but didn't bother to look up. Tiffany would handle it.

"Is he breathing?" He heard the high pitched question from entirely too close, knowing exactly whom had spoken. Forgetting the coffee cup he held, he nearly dumped the contents in his lap as he shifted to sit up and turn. "Yes, I'm breathing." He groused. "Didn't you learn not to sneak up on people at the Academy?" He charged, wishing he'd had one more moments' peace.

"No. Quite the contrary. We learned how to be stealthy at the Academy. What did they teach you? Can you even remember?"

Setting the paper cup aside, scratching his hairline with his free hand, Dublin turned his chair, coming face to face with Darian Gray across the desk. "Ha ha. Isn't there a cloaked picture of you somewhere that I can uncover and be rid of you for good?"

"Ha ha yourself, Dublin. You called me, remember?"

He looked her up and down. Some things had changed, but many were still the same. Dressed in her 'two threads shy of being too tight' tan uniform, Darian Gray was absolutely a woman. The fact that she wore her hair clipped short, in a feminine version of a high and tight, fooled no one. The only thing about her that hinted at being against regulation was the full tuft of shock-red hair that stood above her forehead before cascading to the side, framing her face.

The only trained detective in three counties, Darian was as good as any he'd ever known. No one would ever get him to admit he was glad she had come, but he was mighty glad she was here just the same. She saw things, and noticed things, that didn't seem to be part of the solution, yet somehow always were. That, and her instincts were nearly always spot on. The fact that she understood things, like computers and technology, put her leagues ahead of most of his colleagues in the area. Given what he found at the Culleroy place, he needed her. He wasn't exactly ready for her to know that yet.

"Yes. I did. Don't go thinking I wanna get close or nothing. We ain't dating here. I got something going on that requires your skill set." He verbally sashayed across the desk to where she sat.

"My skill set?! Wasn't it you who said I didn't have one?" She challenged, crossing her arms across her chest.

"Nah. That wasn't me." Dublin waved his hand back and forth. "Must've been Mulrooney over in Walworth. That sounds like something he'd say." Dublin snickered.

Darian tapped her temple. "Nope. It was you. It's here in the vault. I'll never forget it. You want my skill set? You know how to earn it."

"Don't be like that." Dublin slumped. "Can't you just do it because it needs doing?"

Before she could answer, Dublin heard the back door slam, and the heavy footfalls of Bud coming up the hall. "Hey Dub, did you know there's a Stewart County…" He pulled up short as he reached the door. "Oh hey, Darian. What are you doing here?"

Darian looked from Bud to Dublin as she sat down. "You didn't tell your team you called me?"

Dublin closed his eyes so he could roll them hard without the repercussions. "No. Not yet. I guess the cat's out of the bag now."

Darian scoffed. She leaned her elbow on the chair arm, shifting her weight as she turned to address Bud. "Because your boy, Dub…" She emphasized the shortened call, "asked me to come. He was just about to tell me what it is that's got his nuts in the noose tight enough to need my assistance. Why don't you pull up a chair so he can tell us both." She finished glancing sideways to Dublin with her challenge.

"Nah, I'm good here in the doorway. But I'll listen." Bud added as he leaned against the jam.

Dublin was sorry before, when he had told Tiffany to call Darian. He was sorry and smarting now. "First off, nobody's got my nuts nowhere." He commanded. "Second off," he slapped his hand on the desk for emphasis, "We've got a stack of computers high as the garage door out there. If we're lucky, one of them can tell us more about the body we've got in the morgue. Or at maybe, why it's there. I don't do computers. Bud is great with latents, and particulates, but technology isn't his deal either. I'd like to close this case before another body shows up. Does that sound like something you could get involved with helping?" He charged Darian verbally, matching his words with a hard glare.

Darian didn't miss a thing. "Another? Body? How many have you got?"

Dublin looked at Bud who shrugged, before looking back at Darian to answer. "Two. Cal says the second one is responsible for the first one. Which is a really nice little bow to put on that package, but it doesn't tell us anything about why, or why the second one is there."

Darian managed to keep her mouth from dropping open, but Dublin noticed it was a Herculean effort. "Go ahead." He waved her on. "I know you've got questions. Let 'er rip."

"Two bodies?"

"Yes."

"And the second decedent killed the first?"

"Yes."

"You're sure?"

"Cal is." Dublin replied, changing the trajectory of the conversation from inquisition and one word replies to slow the pace of the exchange.

"Based on?"

"Multiple factors." Dublin began. "Ligature marks. Epithelial cells. Late postmortem bruising that matches victim number two's hands."

Darian nodded. "Sounds too tight and too tidy."

Dublin noticed she had shifted in her chair and was leaning forward, a sure sign that he had her on board, or nearly so. "Next?"

"And body number two?"

"Different MO. Same results, different cause. Also, the owner of the aforementioned stack of computers. Sick son of a gun if you ask me based on what was found in his home."

Darian's eyebrows shot up. "Would that be the flashing yard sale sign of crime scene tape out on old 43?"

"It would."

"It's remote." She offered in an odd tone.

Dublin nodded. "Based on what we found, for good reason. St. Louis has the worst of it."

Darian whistled. "You called me... And St. Louis? Eric, what the hell is going on here?"

It irked him that she used his first name. "That's what we need to find out. Fast."

Darian nodded, and stood up. "Take me to the computers, by way of the coffee pot if you don't mind. I'll get started right now."

SWOLLEN BANK

The garage space at the station was converted into Darian's makeshift office. Folding tables were set in a U-shape to accommodate all the computers being accessible from one central seat. They were in the process of taping down extension cords and power strips when Gunner came in.

"Don't shoot the messen... Well hello." He shifted conversations when he noticed Darian.

Dublin groaned. "What's the message?" He asked dryly, dusting his hands and knees as he rose.

Gunner hesitated. "You sure I should talk about this in front of a lady?"

Darian barked out hard laughter as she turned, pointing to her badge. "I'm pretty sure it's okay, kid."

"Kid!?!" Gunner gasped. "You can't possibly..."

"Just spit it out already." Dublin interjected.

"Sorry boss." Gunner shrugged. "We've got another one."

"Are you flipping kidding me?!" Dublin screamed. "It's the middle of the afternoon. How do you have a new one now?"

Gunner shuffled his feet. "Well, see... It's... It rained."

"Not today it didn't." Dublin shouted.

Gunner's clothes all of a sudden felt too small. He pulled at his collar, and the button line of his shirt, trying to get air in so he could reply. "No. Not today. But it did rain. And, when it rains, the pond level rises. And..."

Dublin closed his eyes and exhaled. "You're saying it's in the water." He stated more than asked.

"Yes, sir."

"Fabulous."

"Let's go." Darian cut to the chase.

"No. You stay." Dublin countered, rising. "The sooner you get to work on these, hopefully the sooner this pile up ends. If we can avoid it, I'd like not to have to call the state in on this."

"Party pooper." Darian countered, dropping back into the chair to resume booting up the systems.

"Bud," Dublin began as he turned. "Call Hannity and tell him to meet me out there. Then, call Cal."

"On it."

Squaring his focus back on Gunner. "Let's go."

EJ was waiting by the pond, not far from where they'd found the boy. A small rowboat was tied to a tent stake at the shoreline, and he was already in the snowsuit they used for messy disinterments. "This one doesn't look too good." He called as Dublin approached with Gunner.

"In the water?" Dublin countered mid-stride. "I'd bet not."

Before they managed half the distance to EJ, a voice called from back near the cruiser, making Dublin tense.

"Oh Sheriff…Sheriff? Sheriff Dublin… A moment please."

Dublin groaned as he pivoted on his heel to face her. "Vivika, now is not a good time."

"I see that." She replied brightly, quickly closing the distance between them. "But, as you have no good time any time for me, this will have to do. What can you tell us? Is it true there's another body? Have you identified the boy? Why is there crime scene tape all over a property up on old 43? There are more questions, then answers. Not that you've given any answers yet. You should make a statement before the town draws their own conclusions." She dictated.

Dublin pushed her hand with the small voice recorder away from his face. "I have no comment. It is an ongoing investigation. Tell the town that, instead of the inflammatory hype you've been spewing. As soon as there is something to tell, that is worth telling, we will. Now, if you don't mind…" He ushered a hand, trying to direct her back to her car. "It's not a good time."

He was surprised when she took the hint, but not surprised when her retreat was only to the road. He could see her making notes as she put a cell phone to her ear. They needed to work quickly. He knew without a doubt, there was more company coming, and soon.

"How fast can you get a tent set up?" He asked Gunner as they resumed their approach to EJ.

Gunner looked between the road and the pond. "Not

fast enough. And, not one big enough to obscure the scene."

Dublin pulled out his cell phone, hitting the speed dial for HQ. When the call connected, he didn't give Tiffany a chance to finish the greeting. "Get Bud out here. Tell him we need miles of crime scene tape if we hope to keep the crowd back. Tell him to double-time it, I'm starting the clock."

A few steps off from EJ, Dublin dropped his voice. "Listen, we need to secure this area before we do anything else. The body is in the water, we're going to have a mess anyway. Gunner, I need you to bring a tent, two if you've got them. Set them up side-by-side, here…" He pointed to the stretch of land they had just come across. "As soon as Bud arrives, have him pull tape from the tents at least two hundred yards north and south, then all the way to the river bed on both ends beyond the pond. The best we can do now is force anyone who comes to need binoculars, or a long-range lens to see anything. Do it now."

EJ's eyebrows had lifted, and lifted some more as Dublin gave the directions. "You really think that's going to be enough?" He asked, sounding skeptical.

"Nope. Not even close. But it's the best we can do. Once the area is set off, you can retrieve the body."

Thirty, long, excruciating minutes later, the tents were up, the tape was set, and the crowd was growing. Word traveled fast in a small town.

"You're up." He head canted toward the pond, speaking to EJ. "Anything you can do to diminish the body being seen would be appreciated."

EJ grinned, pulling an inflatable raft from his pocket. "I'm on it."

Dublin's confusion showed. "What's that for?"

"Well..." EJ began, nodding to himself as he laid out his intentions. "I figure, if I can get this under the body, cover it, and pull it along the side of the rowboat, keeping the rowboat ahead of the float, nobody is going to see much until I get to shore."

"Do you think you can manage that on your own?" Dublin asked, unwilling to hope it could work.

"Not even a little." EJ shook his head negatively. Looking past Dublin, his smile returned. "Either you, Gunner, or Cal is going to have to help me. I've got another snowsuit in the boat."

Dublin's shoulders slumped. He knew he didn't want to be the one to do it. Gunner was certainly capable, but Cal might be the better choice. Depending on how long the body had been in the water, the condition of the corpse could already be compromised. Turning to follow EJ's gaze, he pulled his head back, signaling Cal to come over. "Afraid you might be getting wet this time." He began.

"To tow a body?" Cal asked, sounding incredulous.

"EJ here has an idea about how to keep visibility down. It takes two people."

Cal chuckled. "Oh, I see. So you volunteered me."

Dublin shrugged. "Seems to me like this is your area. And, we have no idea how long the body has been in the water. Tell him your plan, EJ."

Cal listened quietly. When EJ finished, he shook his head. "Nope. That's not how this is going to go. The raft is a good idea, but we're doing it my way. If there's a chance that were going to lose parts, or pieces, let's roll them straight into the body bag to begin with."

Dublin's eyes popped wide. "Do you think you can?"

"If we can get him on a raft, I think we can get them in the bag."

"Give it a shot." Dublin replied. "If we can do this without needing divers would be helpful."

Cal snorted. "Tell me something I didn't already know."

FRIDAY NIGHT LIGHTS

Dublin fell back into his chair with a thump. Word had reached the station that the homecoming game between the Howard Juggernauts and the Lynan Cougars had been canceled amid the growing panic. Through the glass wall to the outer office he could see Vivika's report, complete with video roll of the earlier extrication at the pond. He was thankful the sound didn't carry through the glass.

Darian walked in, deposited a bottle and two rocks glasses on the desk, pouring liberal servings of the deep amber before sliding one to him. She grabbed the second, and dropped into the chair across the desk. He tried to ignore her, fronting that he was actually paying attention to the newscast that turned his stomach. She wasn't fooled.

"It's after six. I doubt anyone would fault you after the week you've had. Bottoms up." She nodded with her head to the glass before him as she spoke.

Dublin roughed the shadow of stubble across his chin. He thought he remembered shaving that morning, though it could well have been yesterday. Leaning back in the chair, he swiveled to face her. "Given the lack of information, you might well be wrong about that. I'm pretty sure everybody faults me right now." He lamented with a huff.

"As if they could do any better." Darian chuckled. "Even the Sheriff gets a little down time."

Dublin snorted. "You'd think so."

"Yes. I would. In fact, even in a one horse town like this, the Sheriff should still get to sleep at night."

Dublin ran both hands through his hair, scratching his nails against his scalp as he pulled them back. "It doesn't work that way."

Darian leaned forward, poured herself a second, and sat back again before she spoke. He could tell by her face she was amused. "This isn't the old West, Eric. You aren't expected to do this by yourself. Cut yourself a little slack."

Dublin threw his hands in the air, letting them fall to slap against his thighs. "Slack? There's no room, or time, for slack. I've got three dead bodies, only one of which I can identify. And, the other two? Hopefully Cal can help with the one from today. But, the kid? I'm no closer to knowing who he is than when we found him. Where are his parents? Why aren't they looking? For all the 'no comments,' Vivika has made it her mission to make sure everyone from here to Chicago knows we have an unidentified kid. And still, nothing. It's exactly like the old West."

Darian smirked. "Why dear sir, surely it cain't be that bad. Just last year we got them fancy flushers out at the rest stop to replace the outhouses. We have come so far." She drawled.

Dublin snorted, shaking his head. "As if indoor plumbing is somehow going to save the day." He chastised, trying not to laugh.

They sat in silence for several long moments. Eventually, unwilling to speak first, Dublin took the glass, tipped it at his lips, taking a sip, letting the burn distract him. He absently noticed a straggler as he set the glass back down. Bending over, he pried the mangled piece of plastic from between the treads of his shoes.

"What's that?" Darian asked as he tossed it into the wastebasket.

"Gunner's teething."

"Come again?" She asked.

"It's a straw." Dublin retorted. "Gunner chews on them…all day long, until he unwraps the next one. I don't know if he's trying to quit smoking, or not start. I've never seen him use dip, only plastic. I think the kid must have stock at McDonald's."

Darian's face screwed up at the explanation. "So how'd you get it in your shoe?"

"Because he's a litter bug." Dublin replied, pulling a small hand sanitizer out of his desk, giving it a hard squeeze, and rubbing his hands together fiercely.

The antiseptic smell of the hand sanitizer filled the room. Dublin grabbed his glass back off the desk, taking a quick sip, but longer inhale of the vapors to clear his nose. Darian watched, but remained silent.

They both jumped when the phone buzzed, lighting up the direct line connection to Cal.

"Dublin." He announced as he put the receiver to his head.

Darian waited, thinking he would put it on speaker, surprised when he didn't. She watched as he nodded to whatever was being said. Usually, the sound carried, but not this time. She would have to wait for Dublin to hang up.

"Well...?" She prodded as he replaced the receiver.

Dublin closed his eyes, shook his head, drew a deep breath, and forced a hard exhale. He locked his gaze on hers as soon as his eyes reopened. "We'll know more in the morning. But, Cal's nearly certain that it's Rychard Murdock."

"The City Councilman?!" Darian stammered.

"The same." Dublin dropped his forehead into his palm. "This just keeps getting better and better. Pass me the bottle. One is not going to cut it today."

WATERLOGGED

The long week got even longer Saturday morning when Dublin reached the morgue. Cal was outside the autopsy room with a fresh jar of nasal paste, and a full body hazmat suit. "You have got to be kidding me." Dublin whined, pulling back from shouting when he felt his eyes twitch at the sound.

"Nope. Not kidding. I've managed to keep the pressure down so the whole body cavity doesn't blow, but many of the skin blisters are developing too quickly for me to catch them all. I figured you wouldn't want to wear him." Cal offered matter-of-factly.

Dublin suited up, fighting with the facemask to get it situated. The thin, plastic face shield that attached to the bridge of the mask was not as flexible as he wanted it to be. It was an effective barrier, but uncomfortable. Realizing he'd forgotten the nasal paste, he had to start over. Slathering a liberal amount under his nose, and on the underside of his nose, he began again, this time remembering to place the mask before putting the head covering on over it. He felt ridiculous, but didn't say so.

"I know what you said last night, but are you absolutely certain this is Murdock?" Dublin queried before they went in.

Cal nodded, pushed the door open with his elbow, and head-called Dublin to follow. "Once I dried the hands out, yes. The fingerprints match. I got the dentals this morning. They match too. It's definitely Murdock."

"Damn." Dublin hissed. "Anything else?" He added belatedly, staring at the draped table.

"Yes. And, you're not gonna like it." Cal said, staring at Dublin.

"I already don't like it." Dublin scoffed. "Tell me. Or, show me. I don't believe you got me all dressed up to go to dinner."

To his credit, Cal only lifted the sheet to show what he needed to show. The autopsy had not formally begun. Dublin was surprised to see that the body was still partially clothed. "I left this on so you could see it. It really wasn't making much difference one way or the other for the overnight." Cal muttered.

Dublin gasped, regretting it immediately as a horrible combination on the air hit his taste buds. "Is that?"

"It is." Cal replied, carefully removing the piece in question as Dublin watched. "Honestly, I can't recall ever seeing a belt like this before. Seeing the same one, on two different victims, can't be a coincidence."

Dublin watched as Cal took the strip of leather over to the mold he had made of the ligature marks on the boy days earlier. Presumably, Cal had taken it out for just this reason. He didn't need Cal to tell him that, it too, was a match. "So, we're back to square one." He verbalized the hard truth they both knew.

"So it would seem." Cal answered as he turned. "But the epithelials from the first make this a possible accomplice, not a replacement."

"Well, that's not good news. Do you happen to have any that might be?" Dublin queried, convinced he didn't want the answer, but knowing he needed to ask.

"I do actually." Cal replied, holding up a finger. "Rychard didn't drown." He said triumphantly.

"He didn't?" Dublin retorted, astonished. "Then why the pond?"

Cal shook his head. "I can't answer that, yet. There's no water in the lungs. I pulled them first, partly to confirm drowning, but also partly to relieve pressure from the chest cavity. They're dry. Dust dry as a matter of fact. If there was soil in the nose, or the wind tunnel, I can't say, they were full of water. But, there was a tidy little clot of dirt in the lungs. He suffocated." Cal announced, sounding victorious.

Dublin's jaw dropped open, but this time he remembered not to inhale. "Another asphyxiation?"

"That would be my diagnosis."

"What are the chances?" Dublin asked, not really asking, only speaking out loud.

"This week?" Cal chuckled.

Dublin stared at the mound under the sheet. He glanced at the drawers behind the square stainless steel doors in the wall, and looked back to the mounded under the sheet. His thoughts were turning a thousand miles a minute, and he was having trouble catching up. He shook his head to try to clear it, only picking up the world of thoughts mid-spin. He hesitated to voice the next question, knowing that the next question had to be asked. "Do you think we have a serial killer?" He queried softly, willing Cal to contradict the possibility.

"Well…" Cal began, his head canted sideways. "I'd say we definitely have something. What we have? I have no idea."

"But, it's possible."

Cal nodded somberly. "At this point? I'd say everything is possible."

STORYTELLER

Back at the station, Dublin made it to curbside, but not much further. For all the precautions, the identity of the latest victim was evidently known, or at least speculated on. The crowd was thick between him and the door. Vivika stood on the curb, ready to intercept his path whichever way around the cruiser he decided to go.

Busily trying to avoid her, he managed to walk smack into, whom he later realized was her accomplice. It wasn't a handheld recorder that was in his face this time, it was a full-fledged microphone, clearly marked with Channel 7 News out of St. Louis. "Sheriff Dublin, Sarah Suzette, Gannett News here, what can you tell us about the death of Rychard Murdock?"

Dublin bit down on his tongue to keep from groaning aloud. "Welcome to Howard Miss Suzette. I have no comments about the ongoing investigation." He managed to reply without snapping, or hissing through his teeth. Considering the matter closed, he pivoted slightly, taking off on a different trajectory to reach the front door.

"But, can you confirm that it is Councilman Murdock?"

She persisted, bending her arm around his shoulder to put the microphone in front of his mouth.

Dublin stopped. He turned, taking a deep breath before he finished. "Again, I have no comments about the ongoing investigation Miss Suzette."

"But..." She began again.

Dublin turned, raised his arm, and waved backwards over his shoulder. "Thank you. Enjoy your stay." He said as he weaved his way through the crowd. The last body before the door was the Mayor who pulled it open, allowed him to pass, and followed him inside, pulling it closed behind them.

"Nice deflection. I would suggest you not use that tactic on me. Where can we talk?" The mayor demanded, his tone brooking no argument.

Dublin gestured toward his office. "This way."

"Don't you have anything more private than this? Everyone can see us through the glass." The Mayor bemoaned.

Dublin shot him his best 'I don't care' look. "We can go down to the jail cells, if that's more to your liking."

"Don't be glib, Eric. I need answers. The media? I understand keeping them at arms-length, but you won't do that with me. If this is Murdock, I need to know."

Dublin took issue with his tone, turning to face him with a glare. "Are you suggesting, Mr. Mayor, that I should allow you to impede an ongoing investigation?" He baited.

The Mayor was eight shades of red before Dublin got to the word 'impede.' "That's not what this is! You know it. This is a disaster. We have a serial killer on our hands."

Dublin shook his head. "No, we don't know that yet. The facts don't support that. We have multiple homicides under suspicious circumstances. As near as we can tell, they are related, though what that relationship is, remains unknown."

The Mayor was obviously aghast. "You cannot possibly be saying that somehow Rychard Murdock is connected to the death of that boy!"

"That's exactly what I'm saying!" Dublin snapped back. "And, it's the last thing that I'm saying. This is an open investigation. Yes, it is Councilman Murdock. Anything else, will have to wait until we know what we are dealing with. For now, you want to help? Keep people calm. A riot will accomplish nothing. Give us time, and room, to do our job, and we will get this resolved. This part, this part right here? Is not helping."

Dublin could tell by the changing expressions across his face that the Mayor was not pleased at being rebuked. Wisely, he kept his next comments to himself. Those, and several others after that which, though Dublin saw them clearly as they were thought, did not to get spoken. When the Mayor finally did reply, he did so with a politician's diplomacy. "I don't know that any of us has that power anymore. This has escalated too quickly, but we will do our best. I trust you will do the same."

Dublin smirked. Beyond the Mayor, through the glass, Darian had entered. Her eye roll and body language announced loudly that she had no more use for the crowd or politician than he did. It was amusing to think they actually had something in common besides blended Scotch. Returning his focus to the man before him, he did his best to match the calm demeanor.

"We are working as quickly as we can. The subsequent

appearance of additional bodies has distracted us from the first victim, but only temporarily. Councilman Murdock will get our full attention, just as the others will, in turn. I have a team from St. Louis working on evidence, and have called in reinforcements from Stewart to help as well. Every available officer, both local, and in the city, are working on this."

"Keep me updated, Eric. This thing is a wild fire waiting to grow up to become an inferno. I for one don't plan to get burned." The Mayor concluded before spinning on his heel and exiting.

Dublin turned away from the glass to make his final comments, certain that someone beyond the doors would be able to read his lips if he didn't. "Nice to see you too, Tom. Come again when you can stay longer."

LIGHTS. CAMERA. ACTION.

Darian hadn't realized she'd dozed off until her head jerked up from the sudden drop off the heel of her hand. She blinked several times, looking around to see if anyone was watching. Eric Dublin, all business that he was, would give her the ribbing of her life if he knew she'd fallen asleep.

She had been combing the computers for hours. Marco Culleroy, or whomever had set up his systems, had layered levels of encryption over levels of encryption. No sooner did she break through one, she'd hit the firewall of another, and lock everything up. She was not willing to raise the white flag however. There was a decent chance that this was beyond her ability, but on the offhand chance that it wasn't, she was determined to break through.

She had been toying earlier with the idea that she could spam one of the email accounts to find a backdoor, except that she hadn't figured out the username, or proxy server that was being used. Official requests had been sent to the primary databases, but nothing had come back yet. She was beating her head against the wall, hoping a Hail Mary would pay off. So far, every pass had been dropped.

From the garage she couldn't see, but by her watch she

was certain the sun had already set. She was starting to shut the systems down for the night when the monitor for the one on the far right blinked on, revealing an active camera feed. Dublin hadn't mentioned any surveillance equipment, and she hadn't been there, but she was willing to bet it was from Culleroy's home.

She scrambled for a moment before she realized she had not set up a shadow system yet to record what was coming in. Left with no alternative, she grabbed her cell phone off the table, clicked on the camera, and slid the radio button to video. It was the only option she had as she chastised herself to set up the shadow system before she left for the night.

As she watched, and recorded, the shadowed figure of a woman she didn't recognize entered the frame. Not knowing the layout, Darian couldn't determine where on the premises the woman was. The image was grainy and dim. Wisely, the individual did not turn on any lights, but the silhouette was clearly female.

Her vantage point was obscured when the woman opened a door and walked through. There was no change to the camera angle. Unfortunately, there was also no sound.

When the woman reemerged, she appeared to be as she had been before she went through the door. Evidently, whatever she was looking for, was not there. Which, raised the question, what was she looking for? Was it something that was already gone, or something they had retrieved when they cleared the house? She would have to ask Eric when he returned. He and Bud had gone to Murdock's home earlier, but had not returned.

The hairs at the nape of her neck stood up. Unable to record, and call out at the same time, she was impotent to act beyond what she was already doing. She wanted desperately to call Dublin and send him to check it out before the woman could leave. It wasn't an option.

If nothing else, there were now several other paths to pursue. She itemized them in her mind. One, who was the woman? Two, where in the house was she, and what was she looking for? Three, was she somehow involved with any of the deaths?

As abruptly as the system had clicked on, it clicked off again. Darian hastily saved the crass video she had recorded and emailed it to herself. That accomplished, she stabbed the touchscreen digits to call Dublin. The first attempt went to voicemail.

On the third call, he came on the line, obviously irritated. "Dublin! What?!"

"Don't snap at me. It's important. Someone was just at the Culleroy property."

"What?!" He demanded.

"I'll explain more later. You need to get out there. Now!" She insisted.

"We are clear across town." He countered.

"Then I'd suggest you use lights and sirens." She snapped back. "There's video surveillance. I just saw them leave. They can't get very far without arousing suspicion. It's worth a shot."

"Male or female?" Dublin demanded, obviously running by the sound of his voice.

"Female. Five foot four or five foot five judging by the doorframe." She countered, trying to remain calm.

"You're sure?" Dublin questioned loudly over the sound of the siren starting up.

"It came across his computer. It has to be."

"You said she just left? Why didn't you call sooner?" He demanded, sounding irritated.

"Because I was recording the images on the screen with my phone."

"Good thought. Stay on it." He said, his voice calming down.

"It's all done but the apprehending, or the identification later. The feed shut down as quickly as it started up. I'm at a dead end here."

"Copy that. We'll figure it out."

"Call me back when you get there. There's something else you need to check out."

"Ten-four."

POCKET

Darian hit the speaker icon on her cell phone before the first ring was finished. "Talk to me." She shouted.

"We are here." Dublin replied, not sounding excited.

"Anything?" Darian asked, hopefully.

"Nothing new." Dublin said. "Not that we can tell anyway. We can check again at first light, but it looks the same as the last time we were out here, except there are a lot more footprints."

"Any that don't look like service shoes?"

"Bud… Take a walk around the perimeter and check for footprints." Dublin directed before coming back online. "I'm going in. Tell me what you saw."

Darian hadn't had a chance to upload the video from her email to see it as she spoke now. "Unfortunately, it was dark, and I don't know the layout to direct you well. It was a small room. There is a door, or maybe a closet?" She asked as much as stated as she tried to recall what she had seen. "I couldn't see into the space through the door, but I got the impression it didn't go anywhere, or very far."

"What does that mean?" Dublin asked, sounding

irritated.

Darian took a breath, trying to calm her voice before responding so Dublin wouldn't hear her floundering. "I don't know. They went through the door, they weren't out of view for very long, before they were back. It was like they were checking something, or looking for something. When they reemerged, I didn't notice anything different, but they definitely went out of frame, off the screen."

"Watch that monitor. I'm going to do a walk-through, tell me if I come on screen." Dublin said, hoping whatever had triggered the relay would do so again.

Darian watched the monitor, all but afraid to breathe. She could hear Dublin walking through the phone, and with each step her anticipation grew. Long moments passed before the monitor finally sprang to life. "There! Stop right there. You are on my screen. Where are you?"

"What do you see?" Dublin asked before answering her question.

Darian snorted. "Unless you want me to describe your ass, turn around and look up." She directed.

Through the phone she heard his irritation, as she watched him turn on the monitor. His face spoke volumes. "I'm in the area where the computers were." He announced, reaching out and clicking on the light.

"That's better." She announced. "Behind you in the corner, that's the door."

"It's a closet. A weird closet, but just a closet. There was nothing in it."

Darian was stumped. Whomever had gone in it before had definitely been doing, or looking for something. If it was empty, they could have discerned that simply by peering in, they didn't. "Any chance there's a shelf, or a panel of some kind? It doesn't make sense for someone to go into an empty closet if it is obviously empty."

She could hear Dublin shuffling around, and tapping the walls. She knew as soon as he did when one of them was hollow. "Well I'll be." She heard him comment.

"You'll be what? Tell me. I can't see you on the monitor." She stammered, perched on the edge of her seat.

Dublin chuckled. She heard scraping through the phone, twitching with excitement at what it could mean. When he reemerged from the closet, his face clearly conveyed the deflation. "There's a pocket wall at the back of the closet over a stand of shelves. There might have been something there once upon a time, but it's empty now. We'll have to dust and see if we can pick up anything. From what I can see, they have been wiped clean, but maybe we'll get lucky."

"Damn." She hissed. "I thought we were onto something."

On the monitor she saw him shrug. "We still could be. We know one thing more than we knew before, so that's something. Now, tell me where the camera is. I don't see anything."

"Really?" Darian queried. To her thinking it should be obvious, but if he couldn't see it, was interesting. "Look up." She directed.

"I am looking up, can you see me?"

"Yes I can see you. You're looking right at me." She answered, trying not to sound annoyed. She watched as his free hand came up. It disappeared before it found the lens. A moment later, her view was blocked. "Go back. You just crossed it." She all but shouted.

"This!?!" He asked as his hand covered the lens again.

"Yes! That's it."

As he pulled his hand back, she saw the astonishment crossed his face. "It's tiny."

"Can you remove it? Maybe we can track it through the transmitter."

"I could..." He began, his face through the monitor displayed he was calculating as he paused. "But, I think I'm going to leave it there. Let's see if anyone else comes looking. We can come back and get it later."

"Your call." She said, not hiding her disappointment.

"Chin up, Gray. We have lots of things to go through. This isn't going anywhere. And, if it does, chances are pretty good that were going to see who takes it."

"Fine."

"We will update you when we get back."

"I'll be waiting." She lamented. "Over and out."

VIDEOTAPE

Darian was just finishing setting up the ghost system, splicing the monitor line to another CPU so she could record if it came on again, when Dublin and Bud walked in. "We brought you presents." Bud announced, carrying a laptop and yet another desktop CPU.

"Yay me." Darian retorted, less than enthusiastically. "I'm going to need another table. At this rate, we're going to need a warehouse soon."

"Any luck?" Dublin asked blankly.

"No, but give me another day or two. If I can't crack it by then, we'll have to get the state boys involved, and I'll owe you dinner."

"That won't be necessary."

"Okay." She retorted brightly. "Then you can owe me dinner."

Dublin glared. "Let's just focus on what we're here for."

"Spoilsport."

Bud chimed in as he set the last of the computer equipment down. "I'll go back at first light and see if I can cast any more prints. There is definitely a smaller set out there that do not appear to be work shoes. There have been so many people coming and going between us and the crew from St. Louis though, I'm not holding out much hope."

"So you guys didn't see anybody?" Darian asked, astonished.

"Not a soul." Dublin began.

"We didn't pass a single car on the way out there either, which is really weird." Bud interjected.

Darian was as stumped as the expressions on Dublin and Bud's faces led her to believe they were. "That's strange. Is there anything nearby that someone could have walked?"

Dublin's unshaved chin was in the odd stage, halfway between five o'clock shadow, and rabid caterpillar. He scratched at it fiercely as he debated. "It certainly wouldn't have been my first choice, but I suppose it could be possible."

"Okay," Darian baited, waiting expectantly. When he didn't continue, she prodded him. "What else is out there? Where could someone have gone to, or come from, that didn't involve the road?"

"I know!" Bud shouted excitedly. "The spillway."

"The what?" Darian queried, not following how a spillway was helpful.

"There's a spillway from a short fork off the Kennesaw River, may be a quarter of a mile across the field, behind the Culleroy house. Getting to it wouldn't be difficult, but it's not a fun climb, even if you know what you're doing, and that's in the daylight. Anyone going that way, would need to know it, to be able to navigate it, and they still might break their neck on the slippery rocks." Dublin replied, staring at Bud as he spoke to Darian. "I can't imagine anyone would go that way." He finished.

"It would be my first choice either, boss. But, in a pinch, if I didn't want to be seen, I might risk it." He replied unapologetically.

"Guess we all know what you're doing in the morning then, huh?" Darian chuckled.

Bud's face bloomed with a mischievous smile. "If I'm right, you can owe me his dinner." He said head jerking toward Dublin.

"Deal." Darian replied with a nod. "I can't help but wonder why the monitor didn't pop on when you guys were there before."

"We pulled the cords." Bud countered, trying to hide his embarrassment. "They were off. We didn't see a problem then."

"Next time you'll know better." Darian teased. "Got anything else? Or are we done for the night?"

"Just a videotape."

"Videotape?! Why didn't you say so before? Where is it from?" Darian queried, holding her hand out for the tape.

"Because it doesn't prove anything, except that Murdock and Culleroy knew each other. That, and they, with a third person we need to identify, evidently have some type of common venture." Dublin announced, laying the tape on the table instead of in her hand. "We found it at Murdock's, stuffed under a chair like it had been stashed in a hurry. We need to go back since we left when you called. That, and we need to identify the third party."

"I'll get on it first thing in the morning." Darian replied. "Maybe we'll get lucky."

"That would be a first."

FUZZY? OR FLAKE-Y

Darian was waiting for the caffeine from her second pot of coffee to catch up and cross the blood brain barrier so she could think. While she waited for the video from her phone to buffer, she popped in the tape Dublin and Bud had retrieved from Murdock's house. She watched it completely through three times, unable to put her finger on what bothered her about it. She set it aside when Dublin walked in.

"Did you sleep?" He asked, snickering. "You look like hell."

"Good morning to you too, Sunshine." She snapped back. "I've been here for a couple of hours. The video from my phone just finished, you want to have a look?" She offered, turning toward the computer to start the replay.

"Is there any more coffee?"

"There's a cup on the counter, it might still be warm. That, or there's probably some burnt with dregs left from yesterday. I didn't make any here yet."

Dublin popped the plastic lid off the cup from the counter, tossing it into the trash as he took a sip. His face scrunched up with distaste. "We have very different definitions of warm." He grumbled, taking another sip.

"Beggars and choosers. I said 'might.' Take it or leave it. Or, go make a pot. I can wait." She replied testily, spinning side to side in the chair as she spoke.

"Fire it up. I'll get a cup in a minute."

The video was severely pixelated on the larger screen. Darian had not had a chance to attempt refocusing it. "You might have time now. This is terrible." She lamented.

"Let it play." He said, leaning against the table opposite the monitor. "How long is it?"

Darian shrugged. "Less than ten minutes."

They watched in silence. The grainy, fuzzy images were poor at best. The trespasser was visible, but not identifiable. Dublin's disposition soured. The scene was exactly as Darian had explained it to be, though they would need to clean up the images to have any hope of identifying who was on them.

"Professional videographer, you are not." He teased.

Darian jerked upright, sloshing coffee across her lap as she did so. She clicked pause on the replay, spinning to the monitor for the VCR. She tapped her fingers impatiently as the tape rewound, finally hitting play after it clicked to a stop. "That's it! That's what I was missing." She announced, triumphantly.

"Care to share?" Dublin chided.

Darian held up her finger, forcing him to wait for her to reveal what had occurred to her. When the tape was ended, she clicked stop and rewind, turning to face him finally. "There are four of them." She all but shouted.

"Four of them, who?" Dublin asked, not following.

Clicking play once again, Darian pointed to the screen as she explained. "There's Culleroy, and Murdock, and then this guy, who we need to identify, right?"

"Right. So?"

"So… Who's holding the camera?"

Dublin's eyes flew wide. "You're right. Someone else knows about this. But who?"

Darian shook her head as she clicked stop on the player once again, freezing the image with the three men toasting. "Whoever they are, they never come in front of the camera, and they never speak. But, there is a fourth. I know it. The camera is not stationary, it moves from person to person, which means someone is holding it."

"I'll be damned." Dublin said wistfully, voicing his disbelief.

"Exactly."

It was early afternoon, and several pots of coffee later, before the images from the video conversion were moderately better, and they tried again. Bud walked in as the feed started, squinting at the screen.

"I'm not sure, but I think that's Breanna." He announced.

Darian hit pause and turned to face him, as Dublin head canted sideways. "Breanna?"

"The size is about right. Is there ever a shot of her face?" Bud queried.

"Interesting you should ask that. If I had to guess, I'd say she knew the camera was there." Darian replied. "Even when she comes back out of the closet, the best we get is a shallow profile."

"Not exactly helpful, is it?" Bud leveled.

"No. Not exactly. Did you have any luck?"

Bud brightened. "As a matter of fact, I did. And, looks like you'll be treating me to dinner."

"I'm intrigued. What did you find?" Darian countered, crossing her arms across her chest.

"Hold on, this is my show." Dublin interjected, mimicking her position. "What did you find?"

Bud chuckled. "The storm cellar doors? The ones we noted hadn't been opened in a while the other day? They've been opened now. There were damp footprints on the top few steps, descending into the house. They are smaller, likely that of a woman. There is an obscure trail of scuffling prints that lead away from the house too."

Dublin shrugged. "If they are shuffling…?"

Bud held up a finger. "I got pictures of the ones on the stairs, and I'm no expert, but I'd say they're a pretty fair match for the slightly clearer pair at the base of the spillway." He grinned.

"That's helpful, but not conclusive." Dublin countered.

"Nope. But blood would be." Bud all but shouted, barely able to contain his excitement.

"You found blood?" Dublin queried, astonished.

"Found it, collected it, and dropped it off to Cal." Bud beamed. He turned to Darian. "Where are we going for dinner?"

"Hold up. Hold up." Dublin cut him short. "You can go to dinner when this is over. Meanwhile," he head canted back to the fuzzy video. "You said you think that's Breanna? Breanna who?"

"Breanna Flake. Carl Strickland's assistant over at Justice."

Dublin's jaw went slack. "Strickland?! I didn't even know he had an assistant."

Bud shrugged. "Maybe she's just part of the secretary pool over there, I can't really say. She always told me she was his assistant."

Dublin pinched the bridge of his nose, shaking his head back and forth. "You have no idea how much I hope you're wrong. If you're right, this thing just got really messy."

Darian's laughter bubbled up and she cackled loudly before she could stop it. "*Just* got messy? Evidently we have very different definitions of messy." She leveled, glaring at Dublin.

"Okay, just got more messy. Better?" Dublin scoffed, clenching his hands to fists and releasing them several times.

"Not grammatically, no. Messier, would be correct."

"Potato. Potato. We've got to bring her in."

"You don't say?" Darian and drooled out, rolling her eyes for effect.

"Yes, smart ass. I do say."

Bud tapped his foot loudly. "You're welcome." He clipped to Dublin as he turned to Darian. "So...dinner?"

"Definitely." She beamed. "How about Ponderosa? They've got a salad bar."

"It's a date." Bud exclaimed.

"No. It's dinner. We ain't dating."

INANIMATE WITNESSES

While they waited for Hannity to come in from his fishing trip to grant the warrant, they continued to work on the pieces they had. Darian was going stir crazy cooped up in the garage. "I have got to get out of here. Can you spare me for a few hours?" She asked, sounding irritated.

"Probably. Where you going?" Dublin asked, not really interested.

"In search of perspective."

"Which means what exactly?" He prodded.

Darian shrugged. "I was thinking that it might be a good idea to go to the scenes we are aware of. Maybe fresh eyes would see something that has been missed."

Dublin roughed his chin, pulling his fingers across his lips as he thought. "Another set of eyes never hurts. Go for it."

Darian was moderately surprised he cut her loose without more objection, but then again, he was probably equally glad to be rid of her. The two had not worked in such close proximity for years, and every time seemed more strained than the last. They had never been intimate, but the tension was certainly there. She knew, as well as he likely did, that nothing would ever come of it, but she liked keeping him on his toes, worrying about the potentials. He'd mentored her at one time. She knew he worried, then and now, about propriety and appearances.

Back then, they might have made a good couple. That once upon a time however was a small window, and all fairytale. She was entirely too high strung, too persistent, and too determined to claw her way to the top for him. He had already been in law enforcement for years when they'd met. Settled in and comfortable with the job to be done, he was not willing to have his feathers ruffled by anyone, never mind an alpha female who wouldn't bend. It didn't matter if there was attraction. The ten year age gap was too big for him.

Being in neighboring counties, their paths crossed often enough. He was the rural to her urban, the calm and controlled to her reckless, and the rules and regulations guy to her out-of-the-box thinking that had fast-tracked her up through the ranks. He was happy in Howard. She wanted more; more bright lights, more big city, and more opportunity to take on new challenges daily instead of patrol, wave, and sit a desk.

Still, for being near polar opposites, they complemented each other in investigations, which was, after all, why he had called for her. She understood things that he had not deigned to learn. She noticed things, like the cameraman from the videotape, that were simple and obvious, but easily overlooked. She knew, without him saying so, that bringing her in to assist, while not at the top of his bucket list, ranked higher on the chain than having the state crawling around his

County, telling him how to run his show. She was actively curbing her gut instincts to charge harder, trying to let him lead. It was a familiar dance. One where her toes smarted often, though seldom broke.

She started at the Howard Community Cemetery. The sprawling lawns were still green, even so late in the season. The color was in contrast, but at the same time complementary, to the blanket of falling leaves that covered the property from the entrance to the far border. She didn't need a guide to find where the bodies had turned up. Not to upset the locals, yellow flags had been used to demarcate the spots instead of leaving strings of crime scene tape.

As she glanced across the yard between the flags, it jumped out to her that the one was farther removed from the others. Starting at the most isolated, she walked around the border of flags, hoping to notice something that had been missed. She didn't find much. In fact, other than the soil having settled from the rains that came between, the shallow gravesite appeared nearly identical to the picture she had seen.

Moving toward the pond, and the other two sets of flags, she was surprised to realize she choked up as she approached the small square, knowing it had to have been the boy. This gravesite was distinctly different from the other. It was significantly shallower, and, if she had to guess, it was rushed.

Where the first grave was more evenly spaced, this one was significantly sloppy. She knew that within the depression were distinctly different depths. She noted now, that even though excavated with care, the widths were not equal either. She struggled to comprehend how the same person had opened both. Surely their process would be the same, regardless of how the initial interment had happened. She would have to think about it.

The third set of flags were near the water's edge, with a stray one tied to the cattails in the center of the pond. It struck her as distinctly odd. First, it wasn't like the body could have been tossed from the shore and lodged in the water weeds, there was no current. Second, she knew from the reports that the victim had not drowned. Why didn't they float?

Third, while the point of egress was obvious from the removal, where was the point of input? There was no obvious slippage along the banks that she could see, and as near as she could discern, it wasn't like the body was elsewhere, and slid in with a water channel that developed during the rains. So, the placement in the pond was intentional, but why? And, the burning question, by whom.

Walking back to the cruiser, she noted how well tended the rest of the cemetery was. It seemed strange to her that anyone would choose it for a body dump. It wasn't like it would possibly go unnoticed. If the initial photograph she had seen were any indication, there was very little doubt that the land had been disturbed. If someone were trying to hide the body, it would make more sense to try to keep it uniform to the area around it. The thought process was baffling.

Approaching the Culleroy property, the difference was dramatic. Where the cemetery was calm and serene, the clapboard house off old 43, wrapped and wound in crime scene tape, screamed from well up the road. There was no doubt to anyone approaching that something was amiss.

The yard, and all access points to the house, were sloppy

with footprints. She could easily discern the crew from St. Louis. They all wore the same manufacturer, and other than wear, the treads were the same. Near the storm cellar doors, she noted the smaller footprints that Bud had photographed and tried to cast before following them out to the spillway. The size and shape definitively indicated female.

Back around front, she absently noticed a tread that didn't match up with the others. Racking her brain, she couldn't recall if it was one that had already been cast and catalogued. She dropped an identification easel next to it and took a photograph. It was obviously a work boot, given the extended width, and deep delineation to the heavily webbed heel. But, there was something odd about it as well. Several of the treads around the outside arch had additional depression points that made no sense. She took two more photographs to ponder them later.

Entering the house, it struck her. While the crew from St. Louis, and the locals wore booties before crossing the threshold, there were no other footprints, or track marks inside. She knew the contents of the house had been sparse, but nowhere in the report had she noted any other pairs of shoes. There were none on the porch, none in the kitchen, and no other tracks or treads that she could see.

Filling the kettle, she set it on the stove to heat while she went through the rest of the house. Nearly everything matched up exactly to how they had been catalogued. She stopped when she reached the small room off the parlor where she knew the camera to be, waving in case anyone was near the computers and saw her. She mouthed "hi." As she left the room, presuming the camera would disengage. She was itching to take it down and try to track the relay. She resisted.

Back in the kitchen, the kettle was whistling. She took a thick towel from the stove rail, dampened it with the hot water, and wiped at the linoleum around the obvious wear patterns in the floor. Hoping to discern whether the owner had walked around in slippers, socks, or barefoot, she came up empty. The linoleum fogged, as she had suspected it would, but revealed nothing. The surface had either been wiped clean, or was too old to give up its secrets.

Her last stop was the Murdock residence. Bud and Eric had been back, having collected everything they deemed suspicious, and were currently sorting through them back at the station. It occurred to Darian as she entered that it was curious that both Culleroy and Murdock were single. The notion that they would have been working around a spouse, girlfriend, or even a housekeeper niggled her brain as significant, though she couldn't say why.

Rychard Murdock was all business. His home and office area within were organized, and detailed specifically. The books on the shelves were arranged by size instead of subject or author, which was visually appealing, but inefficient to anyone who would want to read them. A thought startled her. Murdock was living under false pretenses. His shelves were filled with elaborate, and expensive volumes, but she would bet money she didn't have that every single spine would crack loudly if she lifted the cover. They were for show. She wondered what else was just for show.

A wet bar in the corner boasted multiple bottles of high-end liquor. She noted with a chuckle that every one of them was still sealed. Tucked at the back, behind the top dollar versions, were rail grade pints with different levels of empty.

She wondered absently just how long the bottles had been there.

Dublin had said that the videotape they found was stashed under a chair. It seemed trite and too convenient. She couldn't help but wonder if it had been planted. She was more determined than ever to figure out who the fourth man was. The third man as well, but the fourth man who never let himself be seen, was her top suspect.

The rest of the home was all an exercise in sleight-of-hand. Bright, shiny, top-of-the-line stood in front for everyone to see and notice, while lesser brands, and bargain knockoffs hid in the background, showing years of use. Darian was certain there was more hidden in this house than had been found yet. But, she'd only asked to escape for a couple of hours, she was pretty much out of time and needed to get back.

Exiting, she shook her head in stunned disbelief. As she descended the stairs, off to the side of the rail, she caught notice of a too familiar boot print. It couldn't be a coincidence. Following the same procedure, she placed another easel like she had with the first, took several photographs, and tucked the thoughts away for later. She needed to check Dublin, Bud, and anyone else's boots who had been to the property to rule them out. It was just a hunch, but the sooner she could make it official rather than speculation, the better.

Back at the cruiser, she grumbled, noticing a mangled bit of white in the tire tread. Looking closer, it was a chewed up straw. She remembered Dublin's comment about Gunner teething, decided she must have picked it up at the cemetery, and left it, hoping it would dislodge on its own. "That's just disgusting." She commented as she climbed into the car and started it up.

"Okay Darian," she began her pep talk, "The answers are there, what are the questions? Time to play match game."

She let her mind wander as she drove back to the station. Like the fourth man from the video, eventually, something would pop up if she left herself open to see it. The question was, how long would it take?

POSITIVE ID

Late Monday, they had their first bit of good news. The third man in the video was identified, and easily located. His name was Wes Kestle. A known pedophile, and on the sex offender registry, his address was a matter of two clicks to obtain once they matched his DMV photograph. They'd need to get cooperation from Mulrooney over in Walworth County. Kestle lived in Lynan, clearly out of jurisdiction. They called Hannity to coordinate the paperwork. They'd follow up on it in the morning.

Meanwhile, Breanna Flake was being brought in. Dublin was itchy to question her, pacing a path from his desk to the glass waiting for Bud to return.

"Settle down, Eric." Darian teased when she saw him. "You're going to give yourself cardiac arrest before she arrives, and miss your opportunity."

Dublin spun around, cracking his thigh against the corner of the desk. "I just want this whole thing to wrap up. And, you should know it gives me the heebs when you use my first name." He waved her off as she scoffed in response.

"Okay. Okay." She acquiesced. "I figured we were long

past formal by now."

"No. We aren't." He cut to the quick. "Did you know I'm retiring at the end of the year?"

"I'd heard that."

"You don't want any of this. Don't fool yourself."

Darian cocked her hip out, crossing her arms across her chest. "Get over yourself, Dublin. We both know this," she motioned with her hand between the two of them, "Is on a fast road to nowhere. I was just having some fun. But, since you are wound so tight, I'll let it go."

Dublin relaxed for all of a second, jerking back to tense as he noticed Bud walk in with Breanna. He head-canted through the glass for her to be taken to the conference room. She wasn't under arrest, yet. Her answers might change that. At the very least, she had unlawful trespass, and possibly impeding an investigation, as potential charges.

Darian was struggling between snickering, fits of giggles, and outright laughter. Dublin glared. "What's so funny?"

"I was just thinking that you haven't changed a bit. You are just as twitchy now to interrogate someone as the first time we met."

Dublin rolled his eyes. "Save memory lane for when we don't have a murderer to catch." He admonished.

"Go get her, Tiger." Darian tossed one last jab before ducking out the door and quick stepping to the garage.

Bud took her place a moment later. "She's all yours, boss."

"Has she said anything?"

"Nope. Not a peep. I'd wager she knows why she's here though." Bud replied with a shrug. "Or at least thinks she does by her demeanor."

Back in the day, Dublin had tried learning Zen breathing as a self-calming, management tool. He'd quit after the first lesson. Suddenly, he wished he had stuck it out, he could use some calm. Applying the one lesson he could remember, he forced himself to breathe in through his nose, and push the air out through his mouth. Several rounds later, he felt no less high strung, but at least he was able to focus. Staring at the files on his desk, he debated. Deciding to try not to put her on the defensive from the first, he left them behind and made his way to the conference room.

"Good afternoon Ms. Flake." He greeted as he entered.

"Sheriff."

"I think we need to have a little talk."

Breanna shrugged.

"Now, I could spin you a long yarn about why you have been brought in, but you are an intelligent woman. I'm willing to wager that you already know." He tried neutral flattery.

"I have a guess."

"What would that be?" He asked softly as he sat across the table from her.

"You're looking for Carl Strickland." She answered matter-of-factly.

Dublin snapped his jaw shut, trying not to give away his surprise. "Why would you say that?"

Her shock at his question was obvious. "You mean, you're not looking for him?"

"I might be." He prodded, not sure where this conversation was going now. "But, that isn't why we brought you in. Tell me, why do you believe we would be looking for him?"

Her jaw dropped open fast. "Because…" She stammered. "He's been missing for over a week now."

This was news to Dublin. Running his thoughts rapidly, he couldn't recall being aware that Strickland was missing. "Interesting. No one has reported that." He offered, trying to cover.

"Are you sure?" She queried, looking skeptical.

Dublin scratched his chin, absently realizing he was becoming the owner of a fairly impressive beard. "If someone has, it hasn't been communicated to me. I would think someone from Justice missing would have merited my awareness."

Her facial expressions faltered as her arms came up and crossed abruptly over her chest. "I would certainly think so. He's an important man." She admonished.

Dublin was faintly aware they were getting off track. The information that Strickland was missing was certainly problematic. It was not, however, why she was here. He needed to redirect the conversation back on track, and her offensive jab might just create the opening to catch her off guard. "Did you think to find him in Marco Culleroy's closet?" He dropped, watching carefully.

"Did I what?!" She replied, her voice on the verge of objection.

"You heard me. And, before you try, don't bother denying it, we have you on surveillance." He added, desperately hoping to keep the grin from his face as he saw his unspoken 'Gotcha.' register across her features before she covered it.

"No."

"No, what?" He prodded.

She released an exasperated sigh before she clarified. "No. I did not hope to find him there."

"Then what?" He asked, sitting back in his seat, crossing his arms across his own chest to mimic her defensive posture.

She stared back at him unblinkingly. Several times, he thought she was going to speak, but she snapped her lips closed as quickly as they opened. She was obviously debating her next words carefully. "I think I need a lawyer."

Dublin fought not to slump. This conversation was officially ended, and he still didn't know why she was there.

Emerging from the conference room, Dublin waited until the door was closed behind him to grit his teeth and hiss the string of cuss words he was barely holding. Looking up, through the glass he could see the television. The mayor was evidently giving a press conference.

"Fabulous." He muttered to no one. "Now what?"

Clearing the far doorway, Tiffany had the sound turned up. As if the go-ahead had been given, the status of Carl Strickland was being announced to anyone watching Channel 10, and likely a few of the others. Dublin groaned loudly. Standing just off the Mayor's left, holding the mic as though they didn't have stands for such things, was Vivika Turnbull, all but preening for the cameras.

"When did this circus start?" Dublin asked.

Tiffany spun in her chair to face him. "No more than a

minute ago. He's not really saying much, only something about Carl Strickland is missing. How is it we didn't know that?" She asked.

"Good question." He said with a nod. "I myself, just found out in the conference room."

"Oh?" Tiffany responded, her eyebrows halfway to her hairline. "Did she happen to share anything else that might be useful?"

Dublin shook his head. "No. She's lawyering up."

"Damn."

"Exactly."

DECOMP

Tuesday quickly deteriorated from hopeful lead, to a bleak yawn into the abyss. With Mulrooney ahead of them, Darian knew the minute she exited the cruiser that Wes Kestle wasn't going to be saying much. She could tell by the look on Dublin's face as it changed, the moment he knew it too.

"You smell that?" He asked with his nose mashed up before he slapped a hand over it.

"Putrefaction." She answered, her lips turned down as her stomach rolled.

"God, I hate the smell of decomp." Dublin announced, turning for the trunk.

"I don't suppose you have a jar of nasal paste handy." Mulrooney said loudly as he approached the back of Dublin's cruiser.

"I certainly hope so." Dublin replied, rifling through the bag of equipment. "If not, we are going to have to go get some before we go any further. If I can smell it from here, we are going to be laid out by the thick of it once the door is opened."

Darian pulled her satchel from the back seat. Flipping

through the pockets as she listened to Dublin cuss as he came up empty. She found her emergency stash. Hopefully, it would be enough. "I've got some." She announced.

"Thank God you brought a woman." Mulroney chuckled. "They are always prepared."

Darian snorted. "I thought that was the Boy Scouts."

Dublin rolled his eyes as Mulrooney's chuckles became loud laughter. "I was a Boy Scout. Nasal paste is not part of being a prepared scout." He commented between belts of snickers, snorts, and outright laughter.

Dublin rolled his eyes as Darian canted her head from side to side studying Mulrooney. "You were a scout? How long ago was that? Can't have been the current century." She teased.

Mulrooney guffawed, his hands coming down on his bent knees as he gasped for air. "What would a young whippersnapper like you know about that?" He chided back.

Darian held her hands up in supplication. "Just calling it like I see it."

"Mmm-hmmm." Dublin interjected skeptically. "If we're done with the mutual admiration society, can we get on with this? That body is only going to get riper."

"Good point." Mulrooney replied, finally catching his breath and getting closer to normal breathing. "Let's get this over with."

Inside, the stench was overwhelming. The house was hotter than an oven. Dublin had little hope they were going to have much that was usable. They found the body, sitting in a soggy recliner, the decomposition well advanced. Considering the late-season warmth, and that the house had been closed up, time of death was going to be a Coroner's call.

Glancing from Darian to Mulrooney, Dublin asked the first of his two most pressing questions. "Is it him?"

Mulrooney shrugged. "I can't say I really knew the man before he looked like this. Now, looking like this, I have no idea."

"Not helpful." Dublin countered. "We've got open cases in Howard, you want to extradite the body to Cal? Or you want your guy to have first crack?" He leveled.

Mulrooney's lips were mashed together, twitching from side to side as he thought. "Well now…" He began. "I'd imagine that the coroner's office, in the interest of being friendly of course," he grinned, "might be feeling neighborly and willing to let Cal have this one."

"Friendly?" Dublin teased. "Somehow I don't think Cal is going to see it that way. But, it might be easier, given the circumstances."

"That's some truth right there." Mulrooney said nodding. Glancing to Darian, he added, "but you can smooth it over with Cal for us, can't you?"

Darian groaned and rolled her eyes. "Oh sure, I see what you think my job here is. Pack the nasal paste, and sweet-talk the corner. I've got news for you old man." She jabbed.

Mulrooney roared. "We don't get to see you nearly enough Darian. You've got spunk. I like that."

"Great." She replied, drawing out the vowels. "Just what every girl wants to hear, spunk."

Dublin went out into the yard to call Cal. Anything to get away from the smell for a minute. Nasal paste was helpful, but it couldn't cover this. Not even close. This body had been here for quite a while. Once Cal was enroute, he returned to find Darian and Mulrooney rifling through the rest of the room. "Got anything worth using?" He asked as he entered.

Darian held up a plastic box she had fished out from the ever-expanding puddle beneath the deceased's chair. "Don't know if it's usable, but we've got another videotape." She commented, dropping it into a plastic evidence bag.

Dublin crossed his arms, bringing his hand up to tap his fingers across his lips. "Is that weird to you, or just me?"

"How so?"

"That it's a videotape. Either, it's old, or this entire group have not fully navigated to the twenty-first century."

Darian's eyes lit. "Oh. I see what you mean. No, it's not just you. Now that I'm thinking about it, it's really strange. Why videotape? At least, if it's current, why videotape? If it's old, it's just old."

Dublin bit the inside of his bottom lip, it was a nasty habit he'd never been able to break. The dark Venus Lake on the surface belied just how often he did so. "Do you think you can save it, or part of it? Or, should I call St. Louis?" He asked, silently willing her to answer the way he wanted.

Darian's head tipped from side to side, her expression screwed up as she hissed in, and then out, a rough sigh. "I don't know. I can try, but I think we need to set the alarm on this one. Twenty-four hours maybe, then we call in the big guns."

Dublin tapped his watch. "Clock's ticking."

Once Cal came and went with the body, they gathered up anything else that was moderately suspicious. Mulrooney left an open invitation for them to come back, promising to have some air cleaners brought in to make the site workable. They strung tape around the perimeter, as well as across all access points. Lastly, they draped a piece across the drive before they left.

Back in the cruiser, Darian had slid behind the wheel. Dublin was not opposed, as his head was spinning from the overwhelming scents they had encountered. Reaching the station, he was averse to taking the pieces in, concerned that the smells would come with. It wasn't an option. Pulling around to the back side by the garage, they opted to leave the items on the drive between the squad car and the building, opening the garage door so they could be observed. Dublin pulled up short when Darian spoke.

"Were you out at the cemetery today?" She queried, an odd expression on her face as he noticed.

"No. Why?"

Reaching down under the steering wheel, she returned to full height with a mangled strip of plastic between her fingers. "Because this was on the floorboard."

Dublin shrugged. "I wonder how long that's been there." He stated, not thinking much of it.

"I wonder indeed."

Dublin shrugged again, cut around the trunk end of the car, and walked into the garage, speaking over his shoulder as he went. "Hard to say really. Gunner leaves those damn things everywhere."

"Maybe you should cite him for it." Darian retorted,

dropping it into the trash near the door.

"Maybe. But, it's kind of like cigarette butts, they are everywhere, and while we know he is an offender, he's not the only one who does it."

"Well, he's the only one I've seen who does it." She snapped back.

Dublin chuckled, returning to where she stood with a large jug of hand sanitizer. "Take a drive through the McDonald's parking lot. Gunner can't possibly be responsible for all of that. Some days, I wonder if straws aren't the new crack."

Darian snorted, looked at the jug of hand sanitizer, and shook her head. "Keep your goo. I'm going to take a shower. That smell is already in the fabric of my uniform. I can't possibly work like this."

Dublin's eyes popped open at the idea. "Good call. I'll meet you back here in an hour. We can leave Bud to watch the stuff."

"Deal."

FULL REPORT

"Another day, another hazmat suit." Dublin shouted to be heard over the respirator. The suit had been waiting for him in the hallway when he reached the morgue Wednesday morning.

Cal looked up from his spot over the body on the table, not standing up. "Yeah, a simple mask and shield weren't going to be enough today."

Dublin was still adjusting to the smell of the tubing that was feeding fresh air into the suit. "This case needs to end. I'm adding new scents to my top ten of never, every day."

Cal chuckled. The sound was muffled by the suit. "I wish I only had ten on my list."

Dublin looked at the body in disgust. It had been bad yesterday. Today, it was nauseating. Laid out on the table, the pool around it was still growing as he observed bits of flesh and muscle drop from the bones. He absently tried to visualize the calendar on his desk, wondering how many days he had left, debating if it was possible this case would be closed before he went. He knew in his heart of hearts there was no way he could hand this off to someone new, but sticking around to finish it was not a better proposition.

"You want to start here?" Cal asked, indicating the body on the table. "Or, I can give you more information on the other three."

Dublin debated. "Would those updates be done here, or could we escape for them?" He asked hopefully.

Cal shrugged. "Tasters choice. Let's start here, then we can leave if you still need to vacate the room."

"If?" Dublin countered, aghast at the idea he would somehow acclimate in anything less than years.

"Okay. Okay." Cal chuckled. "I know you don't want to, but come closer."

Dublin took several deep inhales, not completely convinced that closer proximity wouldn't allow the awful scent profile to permeate his suit. He moved closer, but not too close. "What do you have?"

"Well…" Cal started, moving toward the head. "There's no flesh here to confirm it, but there are three small nick marks along the side of the cervical vertebrae here at the neck. To me, I'd say they are a similar size for an insulin needle that was jabbed too deep."

"Like…?" Dublin tested."

"Yes. Like that."

"You think it's the same person?"

"It could be." Cal shook his head. "I can't say for sure. But it is too similar to be coincidental in my book."

"Mine to." Dublin acknowledged, nodding his head. "Anything else?"

"Adrenaline." Cal commented flatly. "You say he was found where I pulled him from?"

"We didn't touch him once we found him. So, yes. What

you saw, was the same thing we saw. Why?"

Cal brought his hand up to rest on top of the hazmat helmet. "Because, for the levels of adrenaline, I would have guessed activity." He answered, staring at the wall beyond Dublin as he thought. "I suppose it could've been fear…" He added, belatedly.

"So someone scared them to death?" Dublin asked caustically.

Cal took two steps back, leaning his hips against the counter on the far wall. Dropping his hands to rest the heels on either side of his hips, he was speaking to answer, but his tone was questioning. "No, but something boosted the levels. A fight or flight response could do that. The question is, could he?"

"Could he what?" Dublin charged.

"Fight? Or, flee?"

Dublin stared at the Coroner. Realization eventually dawned. "So you mean like, he was scared, and wanted to fight, or wanted to run, but couldn't. Like that?"

"Exactly. Other than the chair he was in, none of the other furniture looked used, and I noticed a good layer of dust on many of the pieces. I can't help but wonder if he was able to move, or just unwilling." Cal rationed.

"Any way to tell?"

"I requested his medical records, but they've got to come over from Walworth. I don't have them yet."

"Okay. Keep me posted. Anything else?" Dublin asked impatiently, more than ready to move away from the body.

"Not yet. I can't rule anything in, or anything out. There's so much tissue damage from the decomposition, all of the results are compromised."

Dublin clapped his hands together. "Moving on then. What else do you have?"

Cal chuckled. "Don't sound so excited." He admonished. "You want to stay yet? Or, we can move to my office."

Dublin pointed to the suit and hood. "If I can get out of this get up, out is preferred. Let's go."

Cal shook his head and snorted. "After you." He hand-waved toward the door.

Even in Cal's office, the smells were oppressive. Dublin almost went back to get into the suit again. Almost. "Any luck on the others? Or just confirmation of what you thought previously?" He opened, hoping this would go quickly.

Cal chuckled, settling into his chair with a large mug of steaming black coffee. He had dropped one on the desk next to Dublin, but Dublin hadn't reached for it yet. "You might want to take that." Cal directed.

"I didn't know I was thirsty." Dublin jabbed.

"Then don't drink it. Just inhale. The scent of coffee, or coffee beans, cleanses the pallet. It'll help with the smells."

Dublin all but tripped over himself reaching for the mug, forcing Cal to laugh loudly, spluttering his recent sip. "Why didn't you say so?" Dublin challenged.

"This many years in? I didn't think I had to." Cal teased. "Guess I know how much you pay attention."

"Let's just get on with this."

"Okay, okay." Cal said, pumping his free hand up and down as he set his mug aside. "Preference on where we start?"

"How about the beginning?" Dublin replied dryly.

"The boy." Cal said somberly. "Still no clue who he is.

I've run his prints, but come up empty. Unfortunately, there isn't a good database for children. Even in the Missing Children's Database, fingerprints are frosting, but never the cake."

"I can't believe no one is missing him." Dublin retorted. "I can't process an unknown child."

"I know." Cal replied, taking a sip before he continued. "What I do know is this, our initial assessment is accurate. His cause of death is asphyxiation by strangulation. Further, I know that it was Marco Culleroy's belt that was used. While the notches of both his and Murdock's match, only his have cells with matching DNA."

"So you're saying..." Dublin tested. "We can safely declare him as the assailant?"

Cal quirked up the corner of his lips. "I would." He answered with an affirmative nod. "I don't know what more we can find. Other than his identity, everything else we can know about how he died, I think we know. We know he was abused. I know...that it was more than once. And, we know he was strangled until he died. He gains nothing now by us digging too far. Close the case so he can rest in peace."

Dublin slumped as he exhaled. "I should be happy that we can close that one part, but somehow I'm not."

"I understand, and I agree." Cal responded, wrapping his fingers around the mug he held, breathing deeply. "I think there something more to it, but I don't know how we will ever find out. And, it doesn't help the boy."

They sat in silence, staring at one another for several long moments. Somehow, it was the least they could offer the child now. Dublin was lost in thought, trying to put together the pieces of everything he had seen or collected so far. Nothing made sense. Or, what made sense, was more awful to consider than the pieces that they knew.

"Next?" Cal asked finally, chuckling when Dublin jumped.

"Next." Dublin relented, reaching for his mug, suddenly needing a drink, though coffee was not on the top list.

"Marco Culleroy, age forty-nine, found buried at Howard Community Cemetery. As previously discussed, he also died of asphyxiation. More accurately, suffocation by oxygen depletion, or aspiration."

"You don't have enough coffee in the building for me to understand that." Dublin retorted, dryly. "In English please, Doc."

"Remember I said he took a breath?" Cal asked, continuing when Dublin nodded. "He took several. Judging by the amount of soil in his lungs, he easily took three or more. Each time, there was less and less oxygen available, but just enough to drag out the inevitable. He suffocated trying to breathe dirt." Cal smirked. "English enough?"

"But why not try to dig himself out? He didn't appear to be stressed, but lying peacefully when we found him."

Cal shook his head. "I'd say it goes back to the insulin. I think he was probably incapacitated at best, or unconscious at worst. An unconscious person underwater drowns with their first breath. Underground, there's still oxygen, it just runs out. If he was alert, but incapacitated, he would've simply gone to sleep."

Dublin growled. "I shouldn't…but that's too simple and peaceful for someone like him."

Cal drew a hand down his face. "I agree. I don't have a way to distinguish his level of alertness however. Cause of death is asphyxiation."

"Next." Dublin prodded.

Cal held up a finger. "I did find fingerprints on his buckle. They aren't his."

"On Culleroy's?" Dublin asked.

"Yes." Cal answered, unhappy at the next piece of information that Dublin would surely ask for.

"Do we know whose they are?"

"They are EJ's." Cal said, wishing he was wrong.

Dublin propped his elbow on the desk, holding his finger aloft, and closing his eyes. "Hang on a minute… Nope, hang on a minute…" His eyes flew wide. "He wasn't wearing gloves."

Cal was momentarily confused. "EJ?"

"Yes." Dublin nodded, closing his eyes again to see it in his mind. "He was wearing work gloves when he started, but he kept dropping the paintbrush he was using so he took them off. He only had one rubber glove in his pocket."

"Maybe." Cal offered, skeptically. "I didn't see that part."

Dublin nodded repeatedly. "I can see it again in my head, but I'll ask him. Next."

"Rychard Murdock, age fifty-two, pulled from the pond at Howard Community Cemetery. Cause of death, strangulation." Cal paused when Dublin's jaw dropped open.

"But you said he had soil in his lungs."

"I did." Cal nodded. "And, he does. But, he also had soil ground between his teeth, almost like it was being fed to him. Cause of death is strangulation, based on two things. One," Cal held up a single finger. "On the ligature marks that appeared once the body dried out, which I'll tell you more about it a second. But, two, by the broken hyoid. His strangulation was violent. There was no water in the lungs because he never took another breath." Cal grinned.

Dublin was tapping his fingers on the desk. "Back to the ligature marks. What about them?"

"Shoot. I was going to show you this in the lab. Do you want to...?"

"No!" Dublin cut him short. "Just tell me."

"The pattern of the ligature marks on Murdock, matched the boy."

Dublin's jaw dropped open and his eyes flew wide. "Same belt? Was it Culleroy?"

Cal was nodding, but switched to shaking his head before Dublin finished. "Same pattern. Different belt. It was his own."

"No!" Dublin countered, shock lacing his voice.

"Yes."

"But he was wearing it."

"Easily replaced after he was dead. Cellular evidence confirms it. Murdock was strangled with his own belt before he was put in the pond."

"Damn." Dublin dropped on a whisper. "That's harsh, strangling a man with his own belt?"

"Right?"

Dublin snapped his fingers. "Any evidence on the belt to tie it to the culprit?"

"Everything I found, only matches the victim."

Dublin whistled, sitting back in his chair. "So, we have four bodies. Two were strangled with matching implements, possibly by the same person, one asphyxiated on dirt, and a fourth that we can't tell anything more about yet except that they had an adrenaline rush. Does that about sum it up?"

Cal held up a finger as he finished a sip and put the mug down. "Just about. Only forgetting the puncture marks that hit the bone on the adrenaline one."

Dublin's elbow was propped on the desk, his forehead resting on an odd angle against his fist. "So potentially..." He rotated his chin forward to look Cal in the eye. "...two, to possibly four perpetrators."

Cal pulled a deep breath in through his nose, letting it out slowly through his mouth, nearly making Dublin laugh for reasons he couldn't voice. "Right now? My money is on two."

"I think you're right."

JUSTICE

Between his ring tone, and the mad vibration against the tabletop, Dublin was jolted awake by the phone. Reaching blindly, he managed to knock it off, rather than retrieve it. Fumbling to bend over, he was too disoriented to recognize that he wasn't seated, but had been sleeping, at home, in bed. He landed on the floor with a hard thump, cracking his head against the nightstand as he fell. Locating the phone, he clicked the on button, not yet fully awake. "Sheriff's office!" He barked into the receiver.

"Sheriff's office?" The caller questioned.

Dublin blinked hard. His eyes felt pasty.

"Hello?" The voice queried. "Sheriff Dublin? Are you there?"

Dublin shook his head, blinking rapidly to clear his vision. His bedroom came into view just as the door flew open and Darian rushed through, gun drawn, wearing little more than one of his old, white, V-neck T-shirts. "I'm here." He managed, shaking his head, trying to get his brain to come online.

"Oh. Okay, good." The voice, which he now recognized

as male, began. "Are you okay? I heard a commotion."

"Who is this?!" Dublin asked, not censoring the harsh tone from his voice as he glared at Darian.

"It's Gunner. Gunner Douglas, Sheriff. Out at the cemetery?"

Dublin groaned, taking a moment to sit up. He pulled a sheet from the bed to cover his early morning wood, not wanting to send the wrong message to Darian. "Gunner? Oh God, Gunner. Please tell me you're not calling at this insanely early hour to tell me there's another body." He directed, trying to keep the question and panic from his voice.

"Not exactly, no." Gunner answered. "And, um, it's nearly ten."

"Thank God." Dublin said, relief thickly woven through his tone.

"Uhhhhhhm..." Gunner hesitated.

Dublin closed his eyes, pinching the bridge of his nose, and pulling his head down. Darian was obviously eavesdropping on the call, but she was distracting him standing there. He couldn't think clearly. The hesitation in Gunner's voice turned his stomach hard. "You are *not* telling me there's another body, right?" He clarified.

The protracted silence from the other end of the line did not instill confidence. "No, Sheriff. There are two."

With Gunner's response, Dublin no longer cared that Darian was standing there, or what she might, or might not, see. He launched from the floor, nearly landing back on his ass trying to stand on the edge of the sheet he had pulled when it shifted. "Tell me you are joking." He demanded, grabbing his head as though doing so would stop the mad spinning that had started as soon as he managed to get vertical.

"No, sir. I'm not."

"Fan-flipping-tastic." Dublin groused, glancing to Darian who had obviously heard. He began giving the standard marching orders for who needed to be called, and in which order, not remembering until near the end that he, or Bud, would need to be the one to make those calls. From the corner of his eye he noticed Darian return her weapon to safe, and mouth to him. He didn't catch any of it.

"I'll make the calls." She repeated, softly, screwing up her face in irritation at having to say it twice.

Dublin nodded to her, remembered he was on the phone, and sat on the bed. "Gunner, you know the drill as well as I do. I'll meet you there." He finally managed.

Dressing quickly, he began shouting through the wall to the guest room before he realized that Darian was already dressed and waiting for him in the hallway. "Oh." He conveyed his shock as he pulled up short just through the doorway. "I didn't…"

"Yes. I'm sure you didn't. I'm faster than you think. Give me some credit. Coffee's already started. We can make the calls on the way." She itemized.

"I'll drop you at the station." He stated, leaving the rest of his comments unspoken when she spun around to face him.

"No. If I heard right, there's two bodies. You can't oversee them both. I'm going with." She declared defiantly.

"We'll just be doing one at a time." He rationalized.

"I don't honestly care, Eric. There are two bodies. Even if they are each done in turn, someone has to be with the other one while the opposite is being dealt with. You can't do both. You are already going there. I'm riding with you. It makes sense that we just go straight there. Are we really going to fight about this?" She challenged, one hand landing on her hip as the other dropped on the counter, her nails clicking as she drummed her fingers.

Dublin thought to himself as he ground his teeth and mashed his lips together. This was exactly why he should have dropped her at a hotel instead of offer his guest room. They had worked late, and cut the tension even later with the remnants of the scotch blend they had opened earlier in the case.

Technically, neither of them should have driven, but he lived two blocks from the station and they had risked it. Driving her out to the One Stop, the only hotel type operation in town, was not significantly different than allowing her to drive back to Stewart. They'd made a choice between bad decision, and worse. The morning brought worse.

They certainly hadn't consumed enough to call either of them drunk, only mildly impaired, but as the billboard was so trite to point out, impaired driving was drunk driving. Coffee in hand, emerging from the house, he felt better instantly. The cruiser was nowhere to be found. Perhaps they had consumed more than he thought and walked. They'd know in about two blocks.

He perked up to realize that by then, she'd already be at the station. As the scenario to play out shifted, his step lightened. It was temporary.

"I'm still going with you." She announced as the cruiser came into view, still parked in the lot at the office.

"Bud can come with me." Dublin countered, not turning his head, or shifting his gaze.

Darian giggled. "I don't see his car, do you?" She pointed out verbally, and with a full sweep of her arm across the landscape before them.

"Fine." He grumbled. "But, I'm calling him. I still need you to finish, or try to finish cracking those computers." He would almost swear he heard her growl in response.

"I will load, and launch, the new algorithms while you make your calls. We can leave and return, probably before they're finished." She chirped.

It was his turn to growl. "You probably can. But, then you could use that time to work on the videotape from Kestle's. The clock is ticking, remember?"

She stopped then, spinning to face him, planting a boot in front of his path so he would have to pause or detour around her. "What is it? You called me in, but you don't want me involved. I'm not a lab rat. I'm not a technician. You want that? Call the state boys in. Or, call St. Louis. I'm sure they'd be happy to come back out and help. You called, and asked me to assist on this case, but you are limiting my access. Is there a problem that you haven't shared yet?" She demanded, her toe starting to tap halfway through.

Dublin was ready to bite back in response until her last question. There was a problem. She was a she, and a damn fine one at that. He couldn't say that, that much was certain. But what? "No, there's no problem."

She folded her arms across her chest, obviously not accepting his answer. "Then what? Because, it makes no sense for you to call me to assist and not let me. I'm not new. I'm not inexperienced. I'm not someone who needs to be protected, or shielded from the gore. Heck, I probably have seen more than you have. It's not like Howard is over run with gangs, or homicides, or any number of the other things that happen between Stewart and St. Louis that I get to see day in, and day out. So what? What could it possibly be?"

Dublin glared, debating his words. "If I tell you, will you shut up about it? Can you hear it, and let it go? Or, am I going to hear about it until I kick you out of my town?"

Darian pulled her head back, obviously perplexed at what Dublin could possibly be considering saying. "I can try." She finally managed.

"No. You either can, or you can't. If you can't, we're done here. We've got two bodies, remember?"

Darian looked him up and down. Everything about his stance, and the set of his face, said he wasn't kidding. She knew when it was time to call. "I can."

"I've been doing this job for a long time. We both know that. But, it's easier to keep up with you, and the developments, if I don't have to catch up first." He stated, stepping around her as he finished, heading for the station.

Darian's eyes flew wide as his comments registered. It was probably as close to a complement as she was going to get from him. She'd do her best to keep it to herself later, pausing in the moment to give herself a punch in the shoulder and a soft, 'Atta girl...' before turning to follow him.

At the cemetery, the scene was already chaotic. Dublin was furious. "Where did all these people come from?!" He demanded, shouting his rage.

"They followed me." Hannity responded, obviously displeased.

"Why?" Dublin asked, drawing out the sound.

"Because I was having breakfast at Mary Lou's." Hannity countered. "You can't exactly get a phone call, slap money down, and dash out, without people wondering what's going on."

Dublin groaned. "Let's get on with this then." He announced, surveying the yard. Two tents were already set, not remotely close to one another. "Where are we starting?"

EJ emerged from the nearer of the two tents, waving them over. When they reached him, he spoke softly, the crowd obviously too close for comfort. "We've got two, as you know. This one is larger, but not by much. It also has more of a mound over it."

"Show me." Dublin countered.

Inside the tent, the domed pile of dirt was significant. Certainly higher than the others had been. "And you say the other doesn't look like this?" Dublin clarified.

"Nope. I'll show you." EJ said, pulling the tent flap back on the far side, holding it open for the others to exit.

Well across the yard, inside the other tent, the fresh grave was more similar to what they had seen before. "Any idea why they are so spread out?"

EJ shrugged. Gunner entered then, followed by Darian, who, Dublin had decided, wouldn't have been willing to stay behind if he demanded it, and allowed her to tagalong.

Looking from face to face once everyone was inside, he asked Gunner the same question. "Guesses why these aren't together?"

"Not a one." Gunner spat back, shaking his head.

EJ flinched when Gunner bent down, pulling one of his discarded straws from the soil as he stood back up. "You have got to stop doing that. Put them in your pocket, throw them in the trash, or just stop. I've got pockets full of those things, and now it's in a grave." He chastised.

Gunner's head dropped. "Sorry."

Dublin rolled his eyes, turning to Hannity. "Preference?"

"Can we do them both at the same time, and be done faster? The crowd is not going to get smaller."

Dublin didn't miss the smirk that Darian stashed quickly. "We can."

EJ perked up. Looking at Gunner, his expression was of a cat who caught a canary. "I've got Blues tickets if you want to take the big one this time." He offered with a wicked grin.

Both Hannity and Dublin chuckled, the sound changing to awkward coughing as Gunner blanched. A full minute later, he finally accepted, knowing he would likely not get another shot to reclaim his seats. "Fine. But I get the girl." He said, head tipping toward Darian.

"Excuse me?" Darian objected. "Girl?"

Gunner blushed. "My apologies. I get the lady. Better?"

"So not even close."

Dublin snickered, muffling the sound with his hand as he tried to play off that he was wiping his mouth. "Any other objection?" He asked.

She looked at the grave in front of them, not having seen the first, "I suppose not."

Once they left, Dublin noticed the odd expression on EJ's face. "What is it?"

EJ pointed to the marker next to the fresh grave. "Nothing. Once upon a time, I knew her."

Dublin held up his hands. "We can easily switch and you can do the other one."

"No. It's okay. Just give me a minute. I need to go get my tools anyway. I didn't grab them when I set up the tents."

They were finally getting started when Dublin heard Darian's call. "Eric! You need to come over here."

Entering the tent, he found her kneeling down by the side of the pile as Gunner worked to excavate it at one end. "What? You haven't exposed anything yet." He stated the obvious, still irritated that she'd used his first name.

"I know that, but look at these. Are these familiar to you?" She asked, pointing to boot prints in the soil.

"They're boot prints."

"Yes, I know that. But see this jagged part, and these extra impressions in the treads?" She pointed. "I've seen this before."

"Where?" He asked, not putting the pieces together yet.

"One of the other crime scenes." She shrugged. "I'll show you back at the office. But, can we cast this, or at least take pictures around both graves before we get too far?" She asked.

"Go for it. You've got a camera."

She snorted, pulling her phone to begin taking pictures, just as Gunner revealed the outline of the head. Dublin had been turning to leave, detouring when Gunner gasped.

"Got something?" He asked, moving to where the

assistant gravedigger was working.

"I will in a minute." Gunner replied, brushing quickly at the loose soil over the face.

"That's..." Dublin began, pulling Darian's attention away from the boot prints.

"Who?" She asked.

"Carl Strickland." He finished.

Darian's eyes popped wide. "From Justice?"

"Yes."

"I'd like to know where he's been." She said sarcastically.

"Why do you say that?" Dublin asked, his brows furrowing as he faced her.

"Cal will probably confirm it, but he's been dead for a while. The skin is wrong for a fresh corpse." Darian stated as though it were obvious.

Dublin turned to look at the face again. There was certainly something odd about it, but he would not have jumped to the same conclusion, not with only the face showing. "I'll tell Hannity. Cal should be here shortly. We'll know more later I guess. First, I want to know who the other body is."

"We've got this one, boss." Gunner countered, taking his brush and resuming the task.

HOLLYWOOD

When Dublin ducked inside the tent where EJ was working, he stopped short. EJ wasn't working. In fact, the gravedigger was on all fours, heaving in the corner of the tent. "What got into him?" He asked Hannity, pulling the flap shut behind him.

"I don't know." Hannity replied with a shrug. "He hasn't said yet. He unearthed that…" He pointed to the side of the grave, "then he jumped up, double timed it to the corner, and began retching."

Dublin squinted to identify what had triggered EJ. He didn't need anyone to explain what he was seeing, once he recognized what he was seeing. It was a hand. A woman's hand. The odd position immediately made him think it had been clawing for the surface. He had to admit, seeing it, he himself felt a little bit sick. Stepping back out, he went again to the other tent, poking his head in instead of entering. "Darian, I need you for just a minute. Gunner, take five."

Darian's eyes went wide, her eyebrows reaching for her hairline as she rose. "What's up?"

"I just want your initial perceptions." He countered,

whispering as they walked to the other tent.

"Okay." She scrunched her brows together in question. "Are you going to tell me more?"

"No. I am going to ask you to observe, and we will discuss it outside the tent. EJ is obviously affected by what we have encountered." He answered, just above a whisper.

Entering again, he held the flap for Darian. EJ was still in the corner, though the vomiting seemed to have ended. She walked the perimeter of the grave, her shoulders slumping over, and her head dropping, as she noticed the hand. Moving from side to side, she studied it from multiple angles. Looking up, she nodded.

Back beyond the canvas, they moved to a point well away from both tents, hopefully well out of earshot. "What do you think?" Dublin queried.

Her head tipped sideways right, then flopped back left. She repeated the action before she responded. "I think it looks like big city. The nails are manicured, and the polish has glitter. The ring is fancy too." She shrugged. "I also think she has not been dead as long as Strickland. The skin still looks soft, not dry like his. I'm not sure I have an answer for why they turned up in the cemetery on the same day, but they are dramatically different corpses." She finished.

Dublin nodded. I agree about the different times of death. That was more what I noticed than her manicure."

"I'm sure Cal can define that more clearly." She offered.

"Agreed." Dublin said scratching his beard. "Shout if you finish first. We need to get this over with, and get these bodies out of here."

"Will do."

125

Returning again, for what he hoped would be the last reentry, Dublin noted that EJ had resumed the job. He was not ill, or didn't seem to be, but Dublin noticed sporadically that he had developed a case of the sniffles. His hand over his mouth, he studied the gravedigger as he worked. Finally, he couldn't help it, he had to ask. "Care to share?"

"It's Callie."

"It's Callie?" Dublin repeated, questioning the response. Something in the back of his mind said that he should understand what he had been told, but the pieces hadn't clicked together yet.

"Callie Faire." EJ stated.

Dublin's eyes flew wide and his jaw dropped open. Glancing sideways, Hannity wore the same expression. "How do you know?" He challenged, hoping the gravedigger was wrong.

EJ rocked back on his heels, kicking his feet out to sit on the ground. He set the brushes aside, dusted his hands, and ran one down his face. "That ring…" He head-canted toward the hand. "I gave it to her." He snorted. "Actually, I gave it to her twice."

Dublin was fumbling and he knew it. "Catch me up here, EJ. I didn't follow that."

EJ hissed out a hard sigh. He drew in an equally loud, deep breath through his nose. "I knew it was perfect when I saw it. It matched the color of her eyes. I wanted to ask her to prom, but it was only homecoming, and…" He shrugged.

"She was dating someone else."

He stopped looking at Dublin then, his eyes cast to the far canvas, though obviously not seeing that either as he spoke. "I couldn't help it. She looked like an angel, even though she was only the Homecoming Queen. She was coming down the steps after getting her crown. I all but tripped over myself trying to give it to her. She must've thought I was a lunatic."

He continued, his voice far away. "She took it, called it a toy, and threw it at me." He chuckled, coming back to present. Glancing at Dublin, he turned his cheek, pointing to a long, slightly different toned scratch across his face near his ear.

"But, you said you gave it to her twice?" Dublin prodded, wanting to know how it was back on her hand now.

EJ licked his lips, coughed, and snuffled loudly. Pointing to the marker he had identified earlier, he began. "That's Emily. Emily Davis. Callie's mother. She died several years ago." He paused, his lips twisted up as he composed himself. "Callie was long gone, making her big debut as an extra in whatever movie she was working on. I didn't expect her to be here for the service. They really hadn't been close, at least not that I knew. I still had the ring, and thought…I thought maybe it would be like Callie was here, so I brought it with me to the service that day. I was going to drop it into the vault when I buried her mom." He looked up, his eyes red rimmed and wet.

"But, fate being cruel," He continued before Dublin found a question to ask. "She was here. Sitting in the front row, by herself, she was here when I walked up. I watched her through the committal service, surprised to see her cry. I was more surprised by how few people were actually present. Not Callie, she stood up and said thank you to the few 'real' friends her mother had. She was the only family here that day."

Dublin shook his head, not able to place Emily Davis in his thoughts. He made a mental note to check the records later. "So you gave her the ring?"

EJ chuckled. "No. Not at first. I was still thinking that I was going to bury it with her mother. I doubted sincerely that Callie had any idea who I was. But, surprise…surprise, when the minister ended, and I came over to lower the casket, she obviously recognized me. She was the only one who stayed. She caught me off guard when she apologized. I didn't expect her to know me, never mind actually speak to me, but she did.

When it came time to close the lid, I hesitated. I couldn't do it. I bought it for Callie, not her mother. I tucked it into my pocket. I figured she'd leave as soon as it was done, but she didn't. She stayed until I tamped the last bit of soil with my shovel, and thanked me. I… I was just doing my job.

She came back every day after that for weeks. Sometimes I saw her, sometimes I didn't. But, I could always tell she'd been there…here." He corrected. "The next time I saw her, other than in the movies, she hunted me down closing another grave. She asked me to take care of her mother since she said no one else here would."

He shrugged. "What could I do? Of course I said 'yes.' She offered me money. I said 'no.' This is my job. She apologized again for being such a wretch to me all those years ago. Sap that I am, I had the ring on me and offered it to her again."

"And she left?" Dublin asked, thinking the story was over when EJ stopped talking.

"No. She hung around for a bit. Hours, not days or anything." He clarified. "She said she had to get back to work. But, before she left, she said she'd keep the ring. She couldn't believe it was real. Said it was the one genuine thing she had left now. She'd never seen a green amethyst before." He shrugged, his lips twisting up hard. "I didn't have the guts to tell her why I chose it."

Dublin was silent, waiting to see if there was anything more. Nothing more came. EJ snuffled several times and picked up the brush again before Dublin interrupted him. "Are you okay to continue?"

EJ snorted derisively. "I'm the gravedigger. This is my cemetery. We compartmentalize our feelings every day here. I can finish this." He responded with words of far more bravado than his wavering voice supported.

Dublin nodded, holding both hands out in soft surrender. "Okay then. But, if that changes, you'll let me know, right?"

"It won't."

PRESS

For the late start to the day, Dublin was exhausted by the time dinner rolled around. Sitting at his desk, he watched the national news through the glass. He wasn't paying much attention, pondering instead as he ate, when the front gates of the Howard Community Cemetery flashed across the screen. He couldn't hear the announcer, but the headline was large and bold. 'Hometown Sweetheart- Dead in a shallow grave.' His bite of roll nearly became a projectile.

"For the love of all that's holy, who the hell has been talking to the press?!" He shouted as he rose from his chair.

Darian came running from the garage at the commotion. "Who are you…?" She began, absently noticing what was left of his dinner on his desk, her hands flying up with a shrug of her shoulders. "Did it occur to you anyone else might be hungry?"

Dublin pointed to the bag on Tiffany's desk out front. "I called you twice. I don't do engraved invitations for dinner. Food's in there. Now, answer me. Who the hell is talking to the press?"

"What are you talking about?" She asked, looking

between him and the bag on Tiffany's desk, not making the connection.

Dublin slammed his open palm down on the desk, pulling it up to the point at the television where the story was just ending with a closing shot the same as it had opened, the front gates of the cemetery. "That! That is what I'm talking about. It's on the freaking national news. Who has been talking to the press?"

Darian's gaze followed his arm to the television beyond the glass wall. She was as shocked as he apparently was. "I have no idea." She said turning back to him, her hands up to preserve the space between them. "I've been with you all day, or stuck back in the garage putting that videotape back together. It wasn't me. Who else could it be?"

Dublin snorted, pivoting on his heel to pace the short length of the glass wall. Turning back, Darian noticed his blood pressure was high as his face was nearly crimson. "Half the ruddy town was out there today. It could be anyone. That's not the problem. We haven't been able to identify who next of kin is, much less have the chance to notify them…and it's on the national news?" He shouted, barely maintaining his composure. "Can this get any worse?"

Darian wanted to comment, but thought better of it. Somehow, his question wasn't really a question. He was mad. She couldn't remember ever seeing him so enraged. Whomever had skipped over the protocol of notifying the family, or allowing them time to be notified, before plastering it across every television in America, had just wandered into the crosshairs of Eric Dublin's keen, accurate, long-range site. Someone was going to be missing a piece of their ass, and very soon. She was just glad it wasn't her.

When the national news ended, she distantly heard the familiar trumpet intro for the Insider. She should have thought faster, but was in containment mode quickly when their lead story was also about the death of Callie Faire. To his credit, host Tyrone Ramius glossed over the details. He also didn't have a wide angle shot, or B-roll of Howard in the story. It wasn't as bad as the world news, but it was bad enough. Darian was concerned that one more story would have Dublin's head exploding, and she'd be cleaning gray matter off the glass.

A long, extraordinarily difficult day had just stretched to infinitely treacherous. With the Hollywood press, and the world news already reporting the story, Howard would become something it had never been, a choice destination. They needed to work fast, faster than they had been, and they'd been going at a pretty quick pace with the number of bodies that had turned up in such a short window. Dublin was going to need her more than ever. She knew it, but was wise enough to keep that insight to herself.

Cal called at ten. Darian hustled Dublin out the back door before the news could open. He had finally calmed down from his earlier outbursts. A repeat performance was not going to help anyone, or anything. If Cal had news, now was a better time than most to go get it.

She was curious when Dublin perked up as they entered the long hall to the autopsy room. As if the doomsday clock had been set back a minute since they'd breached the front door, Dublin's spirits lifted abruptly for no apparent reason. "What gives?" She asked, unable to resist.

"No suit." Dublin chirped, grinning from ear to ear.

"If you're happy, boss, I'm happy. No suit it is." She teased back, not quite following.

He stopped mid-step, grabbing her by the elbow, turning her to face him. "Do you remember how we found Kestle?"

"Yes." She acknowledged.

He lifted one eyebrow as he glared at her. "Three words, Darian. Full. Hazmat. Suit."

She got it then. "Respirator and all?" She queried.

"Now you got it." He winked. "The spacesuit with all the bells and whistles." He nodded. Waving down the empty hallway, he raised his brows. "Do you see any PPE waiting for us?"

She followed his gaze, and returned back to his face with a broad grin. "Why no, I do not."

"Then I'm sure you can understand why I am a happy man right now."

Before she could reply, Cal popped his head out the autopsy room door down the hallway, giving a whistle. "You two planning nuptials, or are you planning to come in anytime soon? I've been watching you since you came through the front door on the monitor. It's late. Let's get this thing over with."

Darian giggled. Dublin groaned. She, because she knew that he would not be amused by Cal's comments. He, because he absolutely wasn't. They quickly made their way to where Cal was waiting, noticing through the window that both bodies were laid out under sheets. To Darian, it was not a surprise. To Dublin, it was a new development. Every other body had been laid out solo.

"Who blabbed?" Cal opened.

Darian's eyes flew wide before she rolled them, landing on Cal with a hard glare. "Nobody knows. I can tell you somebody's in a lot of hot water though." She answered for both of them.

Dublin was fighting with a growl that reverberated his chest at Cal's question. "What she said." He finally managed.

"Got it." Cal replied, moving to the far side of the tables. "Preference?"

"Anyway you want it." Dublin waved him off.

"Let's start with Strickland." Cal said, stepping to the left. "Don't get me wrong," he held up a hand, "both cases are interesting, and very different, but this one intrigues me."

Darian and Dublin sidestepped to the right, taking positions opposite Cal. "If it intrigues you, then I'm impressed. I didn't think that happened anymore." Dublin teased, though only managing to come off sounding acerbic. He hadn't quite gotten past the news story comment yet. As the drape was pulled back, he looked at Carl Strickland from the shoulders up, noticed immediately, and looked up sharply to Cal who was nodding. "Yes. You're seeing that."

"Does it match?"

Darian stomped her foot, holding her hand up between both of them with her fingers splayed. "Hold up! Your game of telephone here is interesting to witness, but your shorthand isn't one I know. What are we talking about?"

Dublin pointed to the ligature marks on Carl Strickland's throat. The welt pattern was familiar to him, and to Cal, from the earlier victims. He presumed, evidently wrongly, that Darian was aware of them already. "Those marks, match ones that were found on the boy, and also on Murdock. They are from a belt, a double prong buckled belt to be precise. Culleroy and Murdock were both wearing one. So far, only Culleroy's has been confirmed as a murder weapon."

Darian's brain caught up. She remembered reading about the ligature marks, but had not seen the pattern. "Okay. I'm with you now. Proceed."

Cal picked up to respond to Dublin's earlier question. "The pattern matches. But it is not from Culleroy, or Murdock's belt."

"Damn." Dublin hissed out harshly.

Cal chuckled. "Don't 'Damn' yet."

Dublin raised his eyebrows. "Yet?"

Cal drew the sheet further down the body. With his trousers still on, Darian and Dublin both gasped to see his belt. Darian recovered first. "Does that one match?"

"Winner winner chicken dinner." Cal chirped.

"I'll be a son of a gun." Dublin muttered. "Any other cells on that?"

Cal shook his head. "I haven't had time to do any extensive testing on it yet. I thought you would enjoy the first revelation."

"I'd enjoy some answers more." Dublin replied, sarcastically.

"I know. I'm sure you would." Cal chattered, flagging his hand up and down for Dublin to wait. "I have some."

"Such as?"

Cal didn't immediately respond. Instead, he reached across the table, wrapped his hands around the upper arm, and pulled, lifting the torso and shoulders off the table. "Can you see under there?"

"It's the same marks." Darian exclaimed.

"It is, but it's also not." Cal countered, setting the body back down. "Same implement, different motion. The marks around the throat were to strangle, the marks along the back, were more of a either whipping motion, or possibly hoisting action."

"Are you saying he was hung?" Dublin challenged, shaking his head. "Shouldn't the neck be broken?"

"Not hanging like a noose. Hoisted...like suspended for a time. Judging by the discoloration, I would guess after death, or very near to it. The skin has lost most of its moisture content, and the bruising is obscure. Lividity would put time of death days ago." Cal summarized.

"How many days ago?" Darian asked. "Where does this fit in the timeline?"

Cal shook his head, obviously not certain yet. "Four days, maybe. It would depend on the conditions. The Kestle body is from about the same time. But, closed up, in the warm house, with no circulation," Cal waved his hand down the length of Strickland's body, "a very different result."

Dublin's face was contorted when Darian noticed it from the corner of her eye. He was processing. When he finally spoke, it was surprisingly succinct. "More tests tomorrow?"

"More tests tomorrow." Cal confirmed.

"Next." Dublin called out as he started to shift to the other table.

Cal pulled the sheet back over Strickland as he moved to Callie. Reaching her, he withdrew the cover to her shoulders, but no further. He looked pointedly at Dublin before he began. "This is going to be very familiar also."

"Ligature or puncture?"

"See for yourself." Cal indicated the throat.

Darian looked, but could see no markings. "I don't see any ligature marks here." She announced.

Dublin was shaking his head. "That's because, there aren't any. See those?" He pointed to several discolored spots along her throat, under and behind her ear.

"Yes."

"Look closer." He instructed.

Darian squinted. She'd seen enough drug overdoses in her time to recognize a needle track. These were different, but not largely so. "I'm guessing these are not self-inflicted."

"I don't believe so." Cal countered. "Judging by the bruising around the entry sites, I would guess by someone else's hand, and forcibly so."

"So what do you think they gave her?" Darian queried, noticing Cal and Dublin exchange a look before Dublin interjected.

"Is it?"

Cal was nodding to Dublin before he answered Darian. "Insulin."

"Insulin?!"

After a brief explanation about the effects of insulin on nondiabetic persons, it made more sense. She still wasn't quite ready to accept it though. "Who would think of giving insulin as a means to murder? I mean really? Who does that? It it's so convoluted, and far-fetched."

Cal snorted. "Who thinks of doing anything to commit a murder, until it happens?' Who thought of using drain cleaner to dissolve bodies until they did? Who thought of glass cleaner as a poison for infants, until it happened? I'm not saying this was calculated, or plotted to happen this way, but it did. At least, it's happened twice already in this case."

Darian's eyes went wide. "I need to catch up on the autopsy reports from these case files. I have been so sidetracked with the technology side, I've missed the human side. My apologies."

Dublin swallowed hard. It wasn't entirely Darian's fault that she didn't have all of this information before they arrived here tonight. In fact, if he was honest with himself, were it not for the news tonight, he likely would have come on his own instead of her driving him across town to the coroner's office. He wasn't too big a man to admit his role. "I've had you focused elsewhere. I'm sure you would have caught this, and kept up had you read the reports. No apologies necessary."

Cal rolled his eyes and snorted. "Now that you too have made up, do you want the rest of what I can tell you? Or do you want that tomorrow too?"

"Just get on with it." Dublin charged. "It's late."

"Okay." Cal nodded, moving the drape to settle at Callie's throat. "I'll test the lungs tomorrow, but, like Culleroy, I don't think she was dead when she was buried. If the perpetrator knew that or not, only they can say. There is soil up her nose, in her throat, and behind the soft palate. There is also dirt under her fingernails.

I think though, unlike Culleroy, she didn't stay unconscious or incapacitated once she was buried. I think she became aware, was able, and tried to claw her way out. She never made it."

Darian closed her eyes. Buried alive had to be one of the

most horrible deaths to contemplate. She didn't know Callie Faire from anyone. She wasn't a television or movie buff to have any kind of facial recognition either. She recognized a young woman though…one who should have had decades left to live. What had she done to deserve so horrid a fate?

CRACKED

Darian stumbled down the hall, trying not to slosh her coffee. By the time they had finished at the coroner's office, and she had driven home, it was well after midnight. The few hours of sleep before driving back, had been restless. She'd struggled repeatedly, waking up gasping for air, her mind's eye showing her being buried alive. Even in a dream state, it was horrible.

Before the sun came up, she knew she wasn't going to get any sleep, so she'd dressed, filled two travel mugs, and headed back to Howard. These cases needed to close, now. Sliding into the chair, she hit the power button on each of the computers. There had to be away in.

Hours later, she heard Tiffany or Dublin up front. She didn't bother to go say 'good morning.' They would have seen her car. She'd hit so many firewalls with Culleroy's systems, she let them boot up, but left them be. Strickland was likely equally security conscious, so she left his laptop, and home computer aside as well. She was hoping to get into Murdock's system. She knew from his home that he was more about impressions than about actual things. Darian hoped it would hold true now for his personal computer, which had come in late yesterday.

On the surface, it appeared to have impressive protections, but they were commercial, not professional. As luck would have it, Darian knew the back door to one of the programs he was running. Once inside, she was shocked, but not overly surprised to find a ridiculous number of unprotected files. Skimming through his contacts, she nearly shouted, "Gotcha!" When she found Strickland and Culleroy in his email addresses.

Interestingly, both addresses used the same, obscure server. She scrolled through the rest of the contact list, looking for anyone else who had the same provider. There were far more than she would have expected.

Moving to her ghost terminal, she accessed the provider, and set up an account. Back at Murdock's computer, she drafted a group email, copying her new address to the blind send. "Some days I even amazed myself." She whispered to no one as she attached a sabotage file, one she'd been given by a computer tech some time ago, into the body of the email.

She was freshly awake when she clicked send, waiting for the computer code to do its worst, and unlock the other computers on the tables around her. In the past, it had taken minutes to hours, but was always worth the wait. Given the level of encryption on several of the machines, she was betting it would be afternoon before they were open.

She hummed along as she turned her attention to the video tape she'd been sporadically working on from the Kestle property. She knew early that most of the frames were going to be severely distorted, or completely unusable.

She was hoping that there would be a few left that could be viewed and helpful. Re-spooling the tape was tedious and time-consuming. It was already severely damaged. Mangling it further might not be possible, but just in case, she worked with soft gloves, millimeter by millimeter to reset it, hoping it might play if she were careful. If not, it would have to be viewed through a microscope, frame by frame. She'd do that if she had to.

When Dublin walked through, she updated him on the progress, as well as her actions with the computer code she'd emailed earlier. It was nearly lunch time. She could eat, but she didn't want to leave. They ordered carryout, watching the screens in anticipation of the moment.

"You're sure this code will work?" Dublin asked, looking skeptical as he threw their lunch trash away.

"It's never let me down yet." She shrugged. "Sometimes it just takes a while. Given the layers of protection on some of these units, I'm almost afraid to know what they are hiding."

"Good point." He acknowledged as he stood. "No chance of a failsafe?"

"It's possible." She admitted. "But, I would bet not. I don't think they ever thought they'd be caught, or compromised. I think they were arrogant, and relied on sophisticated systems to keep their secrets. Arrogance doesn't use a failsafe." She commented.

"Is that the voice of experience?" He teased.

"Ha. Ha. Yes, but not mine. The tech guys boast about being successful because criminals, or people with secrets, never expect someone smarter than their program."

"I hope you're right." Dublin finished, heading back up

to the front offices.

"I do too." Darian replied after he had gone and couldn't hear her.

When the program worked, it worked all at once. Every computer monitor on the desks around her lit up at the same time. Each with the username and password prompt front and center, waiting for her entry.

This time, she did shout. "GOTCHA!!!"

Dublin, Bud, and even Tiffany came at a run. "What's the shouting?" Dublin called as he came through the door.

Darian was waiting. Standing in the midst of the U-shaped tables, her arms crossed across her chest, with a big grin plastered across her face, she stepped aside when the three of them pulled up short seeing the monitors all with the same display. "See for yourself." She announced proudly.

She relished the shock that played across all three of their faces which also held their tongues. Bud recovered first. "You did it?"

"I did."

"Hot damn!" Dublin shouted. "Let's hope it was worth it."

Darian moved from computer to computer keying in the username and password that would grant access to each system. Tiffany returned to the front desk, but Bud and Dublin each knelt down in front of a machine. "What are we looking for?"

Darian couldn't help but giggle. "Everything. Anything. The files are all open now. I'd start in email, or documents." She directed. "Unless you see a file or icon on the desktop that says 'incriminating evidence.'"

"Ha. Ha." Dublin chided.

It took hours, but before they closed out for the night, they had more information than they knew what to do with. Every suspicious email, purchase, or file that referenced one of the other victims was saved and forwarded to a designated email file for accumulation to the case. There were day's-worth of video files that needed to be checked. They would start on them after a good night's sleep, and after the only family member they could find for Callie Faire was notified in the morning.

Darian connected backup drives to each of the systems, and began the dump. By morning, everything from each one of the machines would be secured for the future if it became necessary. There was no way she was risking losing any data now that they had access.

NEXT OF KIN

Darian yawned as Dublin drove out to the home of Kirk Davis. His address was in Howard County, but the house was situated across the line in Walworth. It was a sincerely odd situation, one that Dublin hadn't been aware of. Then again, along the county line, there were any number of properties where the line zigged or zagged to accommodate a lot that was there before the borders were drawn.

Davis had been identified late in the afternoon the previous day, but when the computers all came on together, Bud had shoved the paper in his pocket, not remembering until late into the evening to let Dublin know.

The decision was delicately weighed. On the one hand, the national news had already released Callie's identity. On the other hand, the family should be told in person. Back on the firsthand, was there an appropriate hour to tell someone their loved one had died? Or, if they already knew, would they be angry, or appreciative, at a late night, in person visit.

The vote was cast. Morning it was. Darian and Dublin would go together, uncertain of Mr. Davis's is normal nature, they were prepared for combative, or complete breakdown.

Pulling into the drive, everything about the property was in disrepair. The shutters hung off the window frames by rusted, well-worn hinges that looked like they would give go at any moment as the warped wood swayed in the soft breeze, trading between hitting the house and glancing off the windows. On approach, they noted there were obvious soft spots, and holes in the steps to the door. The door too looked like it could just as easily crumble into a pile of splinters, as remain standing. Darian raised her eyebrows as she took in the scene, turning to Dublin. "Somehow, this is not what I expected."

Dublin chuckled. "What exactly did you expect?"

"Not this."

"Why? This is easily the poorest part of the county. What did you expect to find here?"

Darian clicked her teeth. "I slipped." She admitted. "I presumed it would be nicer, or better maintained. Callie seems to have done reasonably well for herself. I thought it would translate to home."

"Ah." Dublin nodded his understanding. "That was your mistake. According to the records, Callie emancipated herself to get away from her father years ago. Being that her mother is dead, he's the only next of kin, though this is a courtesy more than anything. The legal connection was severed."

"Got it."

At the door, Dublin hesitated. Looking for a solid spot to knock, he opted for the glass, hoping that it would not give way under the pressure. He'd done little more than tap at it, felt it shift, and stopped abruptly. "Kirk Davis!" He shouted loudly. "It's Sheriff Dublin. Can you come to the door please?" He continued at a shout.

They waited for well on two minutes. Nothing happened. Dublin tried again. "Kirk Davis! It's the Sheriff."

Darian carefully stepped back down the stairs. Walking the perimeter, she tried to peer through dirty windows to ascertain if anyone was inside. She could tell the television was on, but from the angle, not if anyone was present, or watching. With no other alternative, she tapped the butt end of her flashlight against the window, hoping to get a response.

Surprisingly, the response she got was not one she would have anticipated. Normally, when a police officer taps against your window unexpectedly, people jump. Not here. She watched as a head peered around the side of a recliner that stood between the window and the television. She couldn't clearly identify much, but she did make eye contact, she thought. She pointed to her badge, and then to the door, shouting through the glass. "Sheriff's office. Let us in."

She was nearly shocked again when the head disappeared back into the chair out of sight, but no one stood up. "Are you kidding me?" She cussed to herself as she tapped on the window again, this time a little bit harder.

When she made eye contact a second time, she upped the game. Her service revolver in hand, she pointed the barrel at her badge then at the individual inside, shouting, to near screaming, through the glass to get them to act. "Open the door! Sheriff's office. This is your last warning."

She would reserve further judgment until they were face-to-face. She didn't know whether to be offended, irritated, or sympathetic when the only response she got was a lazy wave to enter. She marched around to the door in disbelief to advise Dublin. "There's someone inside." She announced as she attempted to navigate the soft stairs.

"So I heard." Dublin chuckled. "If I had to guess, I'd say everyone in both counties heard you."

"Laugh it up. They didn't seem all that impressed that I was screaming for them to open the door."

"Are they going to let us in?" Dublin countered, trying not to laugh at her obvious irritation.

"No." She snorted. "They gave me a wave to come in, so I guess it's up to us."

Inside, the house was in just as much disarray as the exterior, if not more. Darian could almost swear she felt her liver pickling as they entered. They navigated the landmines of broken things, and empty bottles with care, hoping to step on solid patches of floor, though the squeaking and soft feel as they placed their weight left them skeptical.

"Kirk Davis?" Dublin called as they reached the room where the television was.

There was no audible response, but a hand popped up slowly over the back of the recliner. Dublin shifted around to stand between them and the television, while Darian hung back. He asked again when he could finally see the person seated. "Mr. Davis?" He queried.

Still no verbal response, though the seated male nodded his head. He appeared as though he had not left the chair in decades, though he must have at some point, given the pile of empties nearby with no remaining fulls to replace them.

Dublin tried again, not overly hopeful as he took in the red rimmed, glassy eyes of the male before him. "Are you Kirk Davis?"

hic Once again the male nodded. This time his hand came up open in a shrug, as a waft of whiskey reached Dublin.

Dublin shook his head as he glanced at Darian. Left with no alternative, he would make his announcement, but they would have to return later, hoping Mr. Davis was sober to understand the implications of the news. "Mr. Davis, I'm Sheriff Eric Dublin. I'm here to advise you that your daughter…"

"Ain't got no daughter." The male cut him short, surprising Dublin and Darian, who jumped to hear him speak.

"Sir, Callie Faire… Is your daughter, isn't she?"

"Was."

Dublin's eyes flared wide for a moment, understanding dawning. "I apologize. As the only blood relative for Miss Faire, we came to let you know that she is deceased."

Mr. Davis waved Dublin off. "Girl was dead to me years ago."

"I see." Dublin said, genuflecting slightly. "I apologize for disturbing you. We thought you would want to know. We will leave you then."

hic "Hmmph." Was the only response.

Dublin began to retreat the way he had come. He paused mid-step when Darian interrupted, sounding urgent. "Eric!"

Dublin's head jerked up. Darian didn't continue, only nodded toward a photo on the wall. He didn't need blood work or forensics to know who the boy was. Stepping back to his spot in front of the television, he addressed Mr. Davis again. "Is that your son?" He asked, pointing to the photograph on the wall.

Davis glanced sideways, turning his head slightly to follow the direction to the referenced photograph. "Yeah."

"Mr. Davis, where is your son now?"

Davis shrugged, settling back into his original pose. "Must be 'round somewhere."

Dublin was livid. It took him several moments, and deep breaths he wished he hadn't needed to take, to get himself under control. "Mr. Davis, when did you last see your son?"

Davis shrugged.

"Mr. Davis," Dublin pressed. "It's important. When did you last see your son?"

Davis's eyes were glassy and lost. Dublin had no idea if he was present mentally or not. He didn't want to have to put him in the squad car and take him to the tank to wait for answers if he could help it.

"Mr. Davis…" Dublin repeated, his voice slightly louder.

"I heard you." *hic* "what do you want from me?" He bit out.

"Mr. Davis." Dublin spoke sternly. "When did you last see him? I need to know."

Davis was physically startled by the tone, and newly agitated by the questions. Dublin was about to ask a third time when Davis finally spoke in a rush. "I don't know. I traded him off. He ain't mine no more."

Dublin fought the urge to throttle Mr. Davis where he sat. "Traded him to whom?" He asked carefully, enunciating each word. "Traded for what?"

Davis's eyes appeared to roll, but stopped when he focused briefly on Dublin, blinking several times. "Kestle took him for me. Case of shine," he pointed to a stack of bottles in one corner next to the television. "…and entertainment." He concluded in a curious, and unsettling tone, pointing to the opposite corner, and a stack of VCR tapes.

The expression on Darian's face from her position behind the chair was exactly the one Dublin wished he could be wearing. Disbelief was a simple descriptor for it. Looking back at Mr. Davis, Dublin repeated himself. "When?"

Davis shrugged, his head lolling to the side as his eyes closed.

"I can't believe this." Dublin whispered across to Darian. "Get the photograph. I'll grab the tapes. We'll call Bud to come get him. I'm not putting that in my cruiser." He stated, gesturing to Davis who had started to snore.

Outside, the weight crashing down. Dublin moved around the side of the house before it started, but Darian knew by the sounds that his breakfast had just come up. She was intermittently thankful she'd only had coffee. The gut rot was distinct, and distressing, but it wasn't coming back for a repeat visit.

At the car, waiting for Bud to arrive, they were still in shock. "Did he seriously say he traded his son?" Darian asked, not able to process it as a potential reality.

"He did."

"He's obviously drunk as a cork, do you think it's the truth?"

Dublin's lips twitched into an odd grimace. Darian knew he was fighting again not to heave. When he finally got control of himself again, he responded. "I don't want to. But, I'm almost certain that it is."

"And the tapes?" She queried, wondering if Dublin suspected the same thing she did.

151

"I can't bring myself to say it out loud."

Darian nodded. There was no way in her mind she could speak it either. That Davis had called it 'entertainment' somehow made it even worse. "Me either."

"I hope I'm wrong." Dublin said softly as Bud arrived.

"We."

"What?"

"I hope *we* are wrong."

FAMILIAR

The tapes proved to be everything they wished they weren't. The case got a whole lot bigger than Howard abruptly as they watched. Predominantly boys, there were girls in the mix, though few and far between. The common players between cassettes were Marco Culleroy, Rychard Murdock, and Wes Kestle. Given the developments, there was no lingering question about what their mutual business venture involved.

Darian was newly frustrated. Having to sit through the tapes, she wanted to identify the fourth person, hoping they would make a cameo appearance, but kept coming up empty. When she couldn't take it anymore, she went back to the computers. Strickland's, while opened by the code, was more compartmentalized than the others. The email files were minimal, with very few saved in actual mail. Going through the icons on the screen, she figured out why.

Within any given folder, were multiple other files, with subfolders, or links to off-site storage. The links could go anywhere, making them extremely difficult to trace. Given his position, it was likely that Strickland had done so on purpose. If any of the off-site storage facilities were elsewhere, it would require a federal warrant to gain access, easily allowing ample time to destroy anything before it could be obtained. That he was now dead, didn't change the timeline, only the results.

Hours later, she finally stumbled across an embedded file, buried under several other subfolders. It was a video file. Clicking play, her stomach threatened to heave, even as she knew it confirmed him as the fourth person.

She didn't want to watch this any more than the videotapes earlier, but she persisted until the boy's face came into view. There was something very familiar about it, but she couldn't place him. Hitting pause, she left his face on the screen and went to get Dublin.

"You got a second?" She asked from the doorway, trying to remain casual. She would tell him as soon as he saw the video about the connection she'd made, but she wanted him to look without any preconceptions of what he would see.

"About that long. What do you need?"

"Just a quick ID." She dropped nonchalantly.

"On?"

"A face. It's familiar, but I can't place it. Maybe you can." She offered, hopefully.

"Show me."

"Okay. It's in the garage."

Dublin eyed her skeptically. "It's on one of the computers, isn't it?"

She nodded, hoping he could remain neutral now that he knew.

"Okay. Show me." He lamented as he stood to follow.

In the garage, the screen had timed out. Grabbing the mouse, Darian rolled it to bring the image back up. She was hoping she didn't have to click play again. Dublin sat down, staring at the image. "I see what you mean. They are very familiar, but who the heck is that?" Dublin muttered, not speaking to her directly.

Darian fidgeted with her fingernails to avoid answering the question that wasn't posed to her directly. From behind him, she watched Dublin study the image from different angles, nearly walking out when he reached up and scrolled the mouse to the play button. "Have you already watched this?" He interrupted her departure.

"To this point, yes."

"And?" He prodded, not turning to face her.

"And, this is the first clear shot of the boy's face. The rest I'd rather not see again." She admitted.

"Which computer is this?"

"Strickland's."

Dublin's mouth formed an 'O' but no sound came out. "The image is grainy." He finally commented, back on task.

"I think that's because it was converted from a videotape. The quality, and the tracking seem jerky and off. It's like a worn tape that wasn't going to play much longer because it had been run too many times got converted to a video file, but the quality couldn't be restored." She answered the question she presumed he had but had not voiced.

"That theory works for me." Dublin replied. "Logical, and I think, supported by what we are seeing. Someone who specializes might be able to confirm, or give us a more definitive answer."

155

"Do you need me?" Darian abruptly interjected. "I mean, if you're going to hit play on that, I really would rather not watch. I've seen enough. I just can't identify that kid. It's itching at me…like it's teasing me and I should know, but I don't."

Dublin shook his head. "Go work on something else. I'll watch the rest of this, maybe it will click. They are familiar to me as well, but I can't say who it is. Something about it is wrong."

Already up to her eyeballs in videotapes, Darian returned to the one they had retrieved from the Kestle property. Fully re-spooled now, she carefully inserted it into a slow, low-pressure player, hoping the tape would hold. Pushing play, the screen revealed a muddy, unusable blob of frame after frame. Normally, she would be frustrated, but after the last video she had watched, somehow the brown static that played was calming.

The pervading mud gave way to something the shade of pond water that had been stagnant too long before a couple shadowy frames were revealed. Darian squinted, trying to focus on the blurry images. They were gone as quickly as they had appeared, reversing order back to the brown.

Several long minutes later, the anomaly repeated. This time, as the brown lightened in shade, she was ready for it, slowing the tape as the frames cleared. Her eyes widened as she watched, her stomach rolling with disbelief. If this was, what she thought it was, they had just connected the dots.

She wanted to run and tell Dublin, but waited to see if a clearer set of frames came up to make confirmation easier. They did, at a spot she did not want to see. Unfortunately, she no longer had the option to stop, needing to verify how many other places were discernible.

By the time it was done playing, she had four patches. Four small, mostly blurry patches, but she was certain, they matched. Returning to where she had left Dublin, he was no longer there. She went up front to his office, but had to wait for him to conclude a call before she could share her news.

"What's up?" He asked, as he replaced the receiver.

"We've got him."

"Who?"

"Strickland."

"Darian, I think we had him as soon as you found that video file on his computer." Dublin teased.

"No. I mean he's part of it." She announced, continuing when Dublin's didn't verbally respond. "The videotape? The one from Kestle's house? It's the same video. There are only about four places where the frames actually are visible, the rest was obliterated by the puddle, but they match. It's the same one. It connects them. He's the fourth man."

"You're sure?" Dublin challenged.

"I'm positive." Darian nodded. "And I have a theory about something else."

"Do tell."

"The reason the video on the computer is so grainy? It's because it's a copy. I'm not suggesting that it wasn't copied from an overused original, but the one that was used to make the file for the computer, was a copy of the original, not the original itself. That's why the scenes seem to slip." She offered, trying not to gloat at the revelation.

"That makes sense." Dublin replied. "I've got another piece for you."

"Oh?"

"Yes." Dublin nodded toward the phone. "I just got off a call with the feds. I searched the rest of the computer with the name of the video file and got another file to pop up. It's an invoice."

"And…" Darian queried, afraid she already knew the answer, but needing him to say it.

"It was for five hundred copies."

Darian's eyes flew wide as her stomach let go, her lunch coming up in a rush. Not willing to blow chunks across the desk, she turned and ran for it, only making it to the conference room trashcan. She was still dry heaving, fighting torrential crying jags thirty minutes later.

Boots

Darian was still in the porcelain god position over the conference room metal trashcan when a mangled looking, fragrant, pair of boots came into view.

"You okay?" A voice above her asked.

Darian stared at the boots as multiple scenes flashed through her mind, the obvious conclusion clicking into place. Following them up, the green coveralls gave way to an equally green complexion, complete with plastic bolts attached at the throat. She would have chuckled at the block forehead and appliqué scar, if her head would stop spinning details as they sorted neatly into place. "What are you supposed to be?" She asked with a groan as her stomach lurched again.

Gunner looked offended. "I'm Frankenstein's monster. Isn't it obvious?"

Darian closed her eyes, shifting to sit on the floor, but keeping the trashcan close. "Oh. Now that you mention it, yes. Nice costume. Why are you wearing it?"

She had to look away as his blush under the makeup changed his tone to chartreuse. "Well... I was kind of hoping…" He stammered. "That you might be needing someone to take you to the Halloween ball." He finally managed to get out. "I thought maybe… If you saw my costume, you would be impressed, and agree to join me."

Darian snickered, closing her eyes for a moment. "That's very sweet, but I think I need to decline."

"Because you're sick?" He queried.

"No. Because of the case." She replied, opening her eyes to look at the boots again. "I think you need to get new boots." She stated, not quite ready to announce why.

"No. We just got new boots." He replied brightly. "I fished these out of the dumpster for my costume. We only get one new pair per year on the company's dime, but they never last that long." He shrugged. "These," he turned his foot to show her. "We tried to hot glue when they split, but that didn't last. So, EJ used the nail gun on them to hold them together until we could requisition new ones."

Another detail clicked into place at his words. "Do you two wear the same boots, I mean… The same style?"

Gunner was obviously confused. "Sometimes. Not last year, because I don't like the clips."

"Clips?"

"Yeah, clips." He replied, bending over to lift his pant leg to show her. "See these? These are quick clips so you can pop the boots on and off without laces. They are nice for keeping the grounds out of our cars, or the building when we have to go in, but as the leather relaxes, you can't tighten them. I want laces for that."

Darian nodded. The logic was clear. "So, you had clips last year, but not now?"

"No." He countered, obviously confused. "I tried clips a

couple years back, hated them. EJ loves them. But, he couldn't get them this time, and these were too badly compromised for him to wait for them to have his size. He had to get laces this time."

"I see."

Gunner's expression brightened. "Hey... Your color is looking better. You sure you don't want to go?"

"No. I think it's best if I don't. But, I'm afraid I'm going to need to take your boots."

"Dang it! I was just starting to get used to them. You sure?" He lamented.

"I'm sure."

Darian placed the bag with the boots on Dublin's desk. "I know who he is." She announced.

"The boy?" Dublin asked as he looked up. "We figured that out while you were tossing your lunch. It's Kevin Davis."

Darian shook her head violently. "No."

Dublin's brow furrowed. "You mean the other boy? Or, you've identified the perp?"

"Both." Darian replied as she sat across from Dublin. "They're the same person."

"You're sure?"

"I think so." Darian replied, her voice not hiding her internal conflict.

"Obviously I need to know," Dublin began. "But do I want to?"

"Probably not." Darian answered honestly, shaking her head with a frown.

"Can it be someone else?"

"I suppose, but I doubt it."

Dublin exhaled, squeezing his thighs with his hands under the desk where Darian couldn't see. "Okay. Tell me."

"It's EJ."

FRAME THE PUZZLE

EJ saw the cruiser pull in. There were no new bodies, which left one obvious, inevitable conclusion. It was over. It had been over for him for a few days, but evidently the truth, all of it, was going to come out now. He stayed sitting at his desk, debating if he should stay put, or go to them. Dublin was in front of him before he decided.

"EJ, I think we need to talk." Dublin said softly.

By his facial expression, EJ knew Dublin was not on a social call, or happy to be there. He obviously knew all of it, or most of it. The rest was going to come out, time was apparently up. It wasn't going to be easy either way. "I know." Was all he could manage to say in response.

"How this goes now is up to you." Dublin offered. "We can take a ride, we can stay here, or you can turn yourself in." Dublin listed the options, lifting a finger with each. "Right now, you are unequivocally the prime suspect. What comes out as we talk will determine what happens next."

"Not here." EJ countered. "I'll follow you, or you can follow me, but I'm not ready to ride along either. The media is hanging outside the gates ready to pounce. I don't want to give them that satisfaction. Me riding in the back of the car, or heck, even in the front of the car, and I'm on the five o'clock news."

Dublin nodded, understanding clearly. "I get it. Tell you what," he brightened. "How about you and I take a walk across the yard and back. Then, I'll leave, and you can grab some papers and rush to follow me like I forgot something."

"You'd do that for me?" EJ asked, not hiding his astonishment.

Dublin hated this part, the part where it was someone he knew, and liked. "EJ... I've seen so many things through this investigation that I wish I could erase from my memory, but I can't. I know what happened before. If I can give you a small opportunity to preserve some of your dignity, it's the least I can do."

EJ pursed his lips, nodding. He was unable to voice his gratitude, knowing he would break if he tried. "Then, let's take a walk."

As Dublin had laid out, they returned to the shed and he left. EJ made a scramble to flag him down for the cameras, getting in his car, and following a few minutes later. The drive to the station was the longest, and shortest, of his life. Walking in, Dublin was waiting, Detective Darian was with him.

They ushered him to the conference room. He was surprised that he was not placed under arrest. What that meant or didn't, he didn't know. Sitting down, he noticed the black case of a videotape, all but certain he knew which one it was. He was staring at it, startled and jumping when Dublin spoke. "I'm sorry."

EJ was disoriented. "Why are you sorry?"

"For what's on that tape." Dublin began. "I can only imagine what else is out there. I'm sorry that happened to you." He offered.

EJ nodded, glancing between Dublin and Darian. Telling his story in front of her was going to be difficult. He didn't want her to see him as broken, but he realized she'd probably already seen the tapes and it was too late. "I thought it was over." He muttered.

Dublin quirked an eyebrow. "You thought what was over?"

"That." EJ answered, pointing to the tape. "Ten years ago, I beat Marco Culleroy to within an inch of his life for it. He swore he'd stop. I was naïve enough to believe him." He shrugged.

"You should've reported it." Dublin offered flatly.

EJ shook his head 'no.' "The shame was still bigger than the rage. I couldn't have the town look at me, knowing what had happened. I couldn't report it. I had to let it go." EJ countered, rubbing his hands up and down his pant legs.

"What changed?" Darian asked, needing the complete timeline from his perspective.

EJ stared at her before speaking. "We dug up that boy." He answered, his voice cracking. "We dug him up, and I knew. I knew in my gut who was responsible."

"How could you possibly?" Darian countered.

EJ stood and paced to the far wall. Before they recognized his actions, he had unbuttoned his shirt, dropping the collar down his back off his shoulders, revealing the now, all too familiar welt pattern. "How could I not?" He answered to the wall.

Behind him, Darian swallowed hard, hating every

moment to this point, and the ones that were coming. "What did you do?"

Returning to his seat, EJ took a deep breath through his nose and blew it out through his mouth. "I lost my mind."

Dublin nodded, threading his fingers through his hair roughly. "I can imagine. What then?"

"I went to confront him." EJ shrugged. "But, he wasn't alone. Murdock was with him. They were arguing… Arguing about videotapes, and money…and who to grab next." EJ finished on a whisper. "It didn't even faze them that the boy had died." He said, his disbelief obvious.

Darian and Dublin both stayed quiet. A minute or two later, EJ continued. "They were plotting to grab another kid. I couldn't let that happen." He snorted. "Culleroy was so callous, talking about the ones they'd sold, like cattle. Murdock was arguing that they had orders to fill for movies, he wasn't worried about the other part. I couldn't believe it."

EJ looked at Darian. "I couldn't believe it. I never thought of myself as being lucky for getting away, but in that moment I realized it could've been so much worse."

"Worse is a matter of degrees, EJ." She replied. "You were just a kid."

EJ nodded. "Not anymore, I wasn't." He countered flatly, shaking his head. "Not anymore. I followed them. I was stunned when they went to the cemetery. Murdock was pissed, but they were talking about something that got left behind. Maybe the bracelet.

Whatever it was, they stopped looking when they resumed their argument. They were rolling around, throwing punches. At one point, Culleroy was shoving fists full of dirt into Murdock's face. He hit back, but went wide. I almost applauded when Culleroy killed Murdock and tossed him into the pond. Almost. He wasn't the one I wanted dead."

"Murdock wasn't one of your abusers?" Darian asked, rifling through evidence in her mind for the answer.

EJ's stare was chilling. "Not literally. What I can remember of him was always with, or behind the camera."

"Okay." Darian acknowledged, glancing sideways to Dublin as he waved across the table for EJ to continue.

"He was distracted trying to push the body into the thatch of cattails along the far shore. He didn't see me coming." EJ stared at the table. "I wish he'd seen me coming."

He looked up abruptly, shaking his head as he came back to present. "I jabbed him with my insulin pen from behind. Three times, maybe four. I don't remember."

Dublin lifted a finger from the table. "How did you know to use insulin?"

EJ barked out a hard laugh. "I knew about that thanks to him too. Back then…" He pointed to the tape. "One of the other kids got loose. My insulin dose was on the table, and they'd grabbed it and jabbed him with it. I remember seeing his rage before he dropped like a stone, convulsing on the floor. I remember Murdock kicked that kid hard, sending him flying back into the cell beside me.

I remember hoping he was dead then too. A few days later, he wasn't. He tormented the other boy for hours. I can still feel the bite of the bars where I tried to melt into the corner. He was so mad. Screaming and cussing about how it could have killed him. I wished it had."

"And the other boy?" Darian asked softly.

EJ's gaze came up abruptly. "I don't know." He shook

167

his head. "He was there when I went to sleep one night. He was gone when I woke up."

Dublin drug his hand down his face as he inhaled and exhaled deeply. "So, Culleroy killed the boy and Murdock, and you…?"

EJ leaned back in his chair. "I left him in a shallow grave to suffer."

"But, he died." Dublin countered.

"I…" EJ shook his head. "I can't be sad about that."

Dublin nodded. "Then what?"

"Then I found the slip of paper with Kestle's order. I couldn't help it. I had to know if he was one of them, or just a sick customer." EJ swallowed hard. "I knew who he was as soon as I saw him. He liked to watch. Being taped was mortifying, but being watched live, by someone who liked it, was humiliating. I had to wait though."

"Why?" Darian asked before she could censor herself.

"Because Strickland was there."

"Strickland?!" Darian asked, unable to hide her surprise. She had been nearly certain that he was the absent partner. His presence changed her perception.

"I didn't know until then…" EJ began, obviously upset, and growing agitated.

"Didn't know…" Dublin prodded softly.

"Strickland was paying him… Called it an advance. He was there 'acquisitions' man." EJ stammered, his voice quaking as he made finger quotes. "I don't remember…" He looked between Darian and Dublin as he spoke. "How I got there in the first place." He shook his head. "I was just there. Who took me? How they took me? I can't tell you that, I never knew. Listening in? Kestle was responsible for some who ended up where I did. Maybe, even me. I don't know."

"How did you hear this?"

EJ exhaled as his shoulders slumped and his head fell. "I could see through the window that he was watching one of the tapes, one of my tapes. I crawled in through the bedroom window, listening at the door trying to figure out if he was awake, aroused…I don't know, asleep maybe. Before I could make myself crack the door and look, Strickland arrived. I heard the whole thing."

"That must've been difficult." Darian offered, trying to convey how deeply sincere she was, and that they were not just words.

"I was shaking. But," he shuddered as he tried to cast off the chill that had returned. "I knew I couldn't take both of them at the same time. So, I waited. Once Strickland left, I waited for Kestle to get comfortable again, charging through the door when he reached for his zipper." EJ chuckled before he continued.

"At first, I knocked him and his chair clean over. Maybe once upon a time he was fast, but not so much anymore. Or, maybe he never was, which is why they chose kids. But, that night, I was faster. He couldn't get out of the chair before I jabbed him. And, I jabbed him. Again, and again, and again. My insulin pen was empty, and I was still jabbing him.

His eyes were wide. He was screaming, and flailing, and trying to deflect, but it changed to violent seizures somewhere in the middle. It was like that night in the cell all over again."

"Was he alive when you left?" Darian asked.

EJ shook his head. "No. At first, I thought he was unconscious, but he was dead." EJ shrugged. "I sat him back in his chair, and set it up right. I turned up the heat and closed the windows. He wasn't going to grab anyone else, ever again."

"What happened to the advance?"

EJ broke out into hard laughter. "The advance? The advance was a bunch of videotapes and discs. I burned them."

Dublin pointed to the plastic cassette on the table. "We found that one at his place. Why didn't you take it?"

EJ snorted. "I guess I didn't think I had to. I tried to eject it, but his stupid machine was eating the tape. I pulled the cassette out but the tape was caught inside. It came off the rolls and broke in places. I peed on it for good measure. Guess it didn't work." He answered flatly, looking up as he finished.

Dublin was exhausted by the tale, but they couldn't stop now. "What about Strickland?"

"I went after him the next night. I hadn't remembered him before Kestle's." EJ said, tapping his hand against the table. "Maybe I had blocked him out. I don't know. It came back quick though when I did remember. He liked that belt."

His voice got quiet. "I haven't in years, but now, I hear it every night. I hear the holes whistle as they cut through the air before they land, and the sound of his laughter after they connect." He shuddered, looking up. "How do I stop it?" He asked, his voice barely above a whisper.

"I don't know." Darian answered, whispering herself.

"I thought it would go away when he was dead. I thought, if I made him remember, if he had to feel it, and know it personally, it would end. But, it didn't. It doesn't. It only gets worse."

"So, you whipped him." Dublin stated. "You whipped him the way he had whipped you."

EJ nodded.

"Then how did he die?"

"He laughed." EJ replied, his face hardening with his words. "He laughed, and kept laughing. It was like he liked it. Then, after he was done laughing, he was saying things. Things that made me angrier than I already was, and my ears were ringing by then. It drove me to whip him harder. He said he remembered my first time, and about how much money he had made because of me."

EJ shrugged. "I'm sure I killed him, but I don't remember it. I remember his words. I remember the rage. I remember his laughing face in my mind, and then I remember him hanging in his shed, no longer breathing. I stared at him for hours waiting for the relief." EJ shook his head, staring at the table. "It never came." His expression was pure confusion when he looked up. "Why didn't it come? Don't I get closure now?"

Darian and Dublin traded matching confused stares. When they shrugged to one another, EJ snorted, settling back into his chair again.

"Then why Callie?" Darian asked carefully.

EJ's jaw went slack. He pulled it closed, twisting his lips into a hard line as a tear tracked his cheek. "No. I can't." He finally said, shaking his head violently.

"EJ, we know it was you. There are too many coincidences to the other bodies. Tell us why." Dublin urged. "Without the why, it's easy First Degree. With the why, maybe it's not."

EJ glanced between them, obviously debating what to

say, or how to say it. It was a difficult choice. He didn't want to remember the why. He wanted to remember her before. "I… She…" He deteriorated quickly into a shaking mess, tears spilling heavily down his face as he wrapped his arms around himself trying to keep it together. He was exhausted by it before it was over. Dublin and Darien waited patiently, which somehow made it worse.

Swallowing hard, if he was going to get it out, it had to be fast. He took a deep breath, and spilled the tale quickly in a single breath. "Because she was there. With Strickland. She was telling him about how she could take his videos to a producer, or distributor, or someone she knew in Hollywood who could get him a bigger audience.

I confronted her after I dealt with him, and she laughed at me. She told me I was a liar, that it wasn't me in the video, and even if it was, no one would recognize me, or care. She knew a way to make millions.

I told her Strickland was dead, and his tapes were all gone. She wouldn't make a dime off my back with her plan. I was going to walk away, but she didn't stop. She laughed louder and said she already had."

Darian was biting her tongue to keep from crying, or gasping. It was surreal. In her mind, every single death was warranted for what they had put this man through. But, she couldn't say that. When he looked up, she knew the story was over. Every piece of evidence they had, supported his version of the events. The only thing left, was the arrest.

Sheriff Dublin gave an official statement for the first and last time from the entrance of the Howard Community Cemetery. To him, it could have been a White House Press Corps briefing for all the cameras and reporters. He outlined the deaths, and the arrest, glazing over the reasons why. Everything would come out soon enough. There was no way to stop that, but he did not need to drag EJ any further down than the man had already been leveled.

The murders were officially solved, and the county cases officially closed. Sadly, the story wouldn't end there. Though the murders had all taken place locally, because of the larger scope of the situation, the case was moving to a federal jurisdiction. Dublin hoped that when the details all surfaced that there would be lenience for the man who had already suffered so much.

Breanna Flake was on the run. How far she would get before the feds apprehended her, Dublin didn't venture to guess. Once she had lawyered up, and bailed out, he had stopped tracking her. Given everything, he should feel bad about that, but really didn't.

Kirk Davis was being transferred to a state holding facility soon. Dublin would be exponentially glad to be rid of him. His pores still wept alcohol, even so many days later. It would take a year for the cells to be cleared of the stench, though that would not be his problem then.

The news story would play on repeat, likely for the foreseeable future. Dublin hoped that the further it got buried, the sooner folks would forget. He knew he would never forget, which troubled him greatly. There were some things that could not be unseen.

Chuckling, he closed his files and helped Darian pack her car. "I can't thank you enough. Who knows how long this would have hung open without you." He acknowledged when she was nearly ready to leave.

"Gratitude?" She teased. "I'll just keep that to myself. Wouldn't want to ruin your reputation."

"Reputation?" He teased back. "I'm retiring. Who cares?"

"You never know."

"Okay fine." He acquiesced. "Let's go. If my reputation is in peril, I suppose I should take you to dinner and say thank you properly."

Darian batted her lashes, fluttering her hand against her chest. "I always knew you had it in you."

"Yeah? Well, keep it to yourself."

"So dinner makes us even?"

Dublin snorted. "Something like that."

Darian smiled with a nod. "I guess a girl has to take what she can get."

"As if you'd ever settle, Darian."

"I might." She teased, but only a little, and less than he realized.

"No."

"Spoilsport. Take me to dinner before I change my mind. You get to retire. I've got a wrap all the paperwork side of this up. I'd say you owe me a good dinner."

"Ponderosa it is." Dublin announced, laughing robustly for the first time in weeks.

Darian paused the laughter a moment later. "What do you think will happen?" She asked, all kidding aside.

"I don't know." Dublin replied, obviously choking up. "I

hope they call me to testify though. Given what we know, EJ needs someone on his side."

"Sign me up." Darian retorted, nodding vigorously. "Sign me up."

Dublin used the back of his hand to wipe his nose. The day needed to end. "Are we eating or what?" He asked, adding when she nodded. "Good. I'm starving. But, if you get the salad bar too, you're buying. We ain't dating."

EPILOGUE

Darian and Dublin read the same newspaper article, at the same time, in different places. Darian from her office in Stewart, Dublin at his kitchen table, over coffee.

Local sheriff retires with honors

Howard County Sheriff, Eric Dublin, retires after nearly thirty years, culminating his career by solving the biggest case to ever hit the area. With the assistance of Detective Darian Gray, Dublin concluded the investigation of six homicides, only days before leaving office. The duo also cracked open the inner circle responsible for a pedophile and human trafficking operation that had evaded federal investigators for years. That investigation continues.

Sheriff Dublin was unavailable for comment, but Detective Gray offered commentary. "It was my privilege and honor to work side by side, and learn from the Sheriff again. His commitment to the community never faltered, leaving a high bar for his successor to be measured against." Gray stated. The new Sheriff for Howard County has yet to be named.

See Sheriff, page 4.

Darian stopped after the two paragraphs on page one, pleased to see Dublin as the focus. She set the paper aside. Even weeks later, she had numerous reports and filings to make transferring the balance of their findings and observations to the federal team that would pick up the balance of the investigation. She was actively ignoring their request for her to consult.

Dublin shuffled the pages to see the rest of the story, but not before smirking at the intro. He finished reading, poured himself another cup of coffee, and stared out the window. It was time to decide what to do with the rest of his life. Topping the agenda, Kirk Davis's property still fresh in his mind, was getting his own affairs in order, starting with the leaking roof before the next rain.

Intermittently glancing at the paper, now folded next to him on the table, he snickered, wondering if he would ever cross paths with Darian again. The investigation had been full of moments, good ones, and bad ones. In the end though, even he had to admit they made a good team. He said it as soon as he thought it, even though no one else was around to hear it. "Blasted woman. I should have known she'd find a way to get the last word in."

FROM THE AUTHOR

Some of the underlying subject matter here is difficult. It was to write, I'm sure also to read. The details have been left intentionally vague. The horrors of child abuse and human trafficking are very real. I hope one day the will become extinct. This story is complete fiction. No disrespect is intended.

Decades ago, I had the distinct privilege to work with survivors, trying to help them regain some semblance of 'normal' in their quest to find happiness and move past their experiences, even if only for a little while when they were with me.

This message is for them:

It's been thirty years, but I still remember your names and your stories. I see your faces in my mind as they were then. I did not write this to glorify or gloss over the tragedy of human suffering, yours, or anyone else's. Your story has never been mine to share. I have not here. I will not ever. Your secrets are safe, and your confidences secure. I hope you're thriving.

You're always in my heart.

~Savile

ABOUT THE AUTHOR

A lifelong lover of words and reading, Savanah Verte hasn't quite figured out what she wants to write when she grows up. Born and raised in the upper Midwest, Savannah's gypsy spirit and never quit attitude keep her busy and seldom idle. For so many reasons, Savannah considers herself a 'Contemporary Vagabond' when it comes to writing and hopes that others find her diverse offerings as enjoyable to read as they are to write.

As the primary owner and driving force behind Eclectic Bard Books, she considers herself immensely fortunate to see writing from varied perspectives as she endeavors to publish the authors rostered there. Working with other writers, Savannah gets to expand her horizons every day as someone brings a new idea to the table and the brainstorming begins. There is something addictive about the creative process for her and helping other authors embrace their dreams make hers a reality daily.

Follow Savannah:
www.savannahverte.com
www.facebook.com/authorsavannahverte
www.eclecticbardbooks.com/savannahverte

OTHER TITLES BY SAVANNAH VERTE

Viva Zapata & the Magic 8-Ball

The Custos Series:
Book of Time
Book of Change
Book of Mysteries

C.A.S.E. Revelations

Tales in 13 Chapters:
Immortal Deflagration
Immortal Alchemy

Imposs-i-Bella
A Flip-Flopped Fairy Tale

Rogue
Cimmerian Shade box set

Veil Break
(Haunting Savannah box set October 10, 2017)

The Vengelys Series Complete Set
(2017-2018 release pending w/Aedan Byrnes)

Viva Zapata & the Magic 8-Ball

Sometimes, what happens in Vegas can't stay in Vegas.

Four women gather in Sin City for a long weekend. Somewhere between the glitzy casinos and the small-hours-of-the-morning truths, they discover that the game of life doesn't play by the house rules.

Three days, one Mexican revolutionary, and one Magic 8-Ball later, the women realize that with friends by your side, you can play any hand that life deals…and win.

Available on eBook at amazon, and in print at fine booksellers everywhere:
http://www.amzn.com/B01217QQVQ

Viva Zapata & the Magic 8-Ball
EXCERPT

Concentrate and ask again

Two fears collided as Abi Stewart rounded the corner of baggage carousel seven at McCarran airport. The first was a deep, long standing fear that her friends had not come and she would once again be standing alone. The second surprised her as a new insecurity reared up and stole her breath. It was a nervous fear as she looked up and noticed the three beauties at the far end. Not only had they come, but these were her companions for the weekend.

A lose or lose notion reared its ugly head and threatened to wipe the smile from her face. She forced herself to breathe through her nose as she held her grin in place and started toward the trio. The returning radiant smiles confirmed fear number two of the morning. She would not be standing alone, they were here, and this was them.

Her father had always told her that achieving greatness begins with the smallest disciplines. She had often found that keeping her composure in spite of her internal struggle required immense discipline. This time would be no exception.

Why she did this to herself was anyone's guess. In the span of distance from one end of the baggage wheel to the other she had assessed her clothing as inferior, inspected her makeup in her mind, and determined she needed better shoes. The queen of self-sabotage had evidently come along for the girl's weekend too. It was not without great effort that she managed to arrive where the others stood with her smile still in place.

"You all failed to mention that you were gorgeous." Abi began, hoping to move past her own feelings of awkwardness quickly with humor.

The tan, brunette, Marilyn Monroe curve twin, who had to be Margo, scoffed it off while the petite, maybe size zero soaking wet Meredith, blushed quietly. Only Dani, who actually was a model, looked bored and put off by the assessment and her opening volley. "Puh-leeze."

Abi tried humor again. "I'm just saying it so it's been said. I've seen your faces, but damn, really? You might have warned a girl."

Meredith chimed in, "I think you made my day. Are we set?"

"No, haven't seen my bag drop yet. You guys been here long?" Abi asked.

Dani was busily bopping her head and bouncing a hip making an 'Nnn-cha' sound over and over again as she swayed back and forth. Abi wasn't sure if it was code for, 'Yes we have. No, I'm bored.' Or 'Let me know when we're ready to move, I can't stand still.' Then again, it almost seemed like she was rocking out to a song only she could hear, Abi certainly couldn't.

Margo finally answered, breaking Abi's stare at the blonde amazon gyrating in front of her. "Nah, not long. I just arrived a bit ago actually. These two were already here, though I nearly missed Meredith for the group around them when I landed."

Meredith rolled her eyes. "Ha. Ha. Notice she didn't say she nearly missed 'us', just me."

Abi's eyes were wide. "Were you really surrounded?"

Meredith thumbed toward the six foot plus blonde to her left in jeans, t-shirt and a straw hat. "Even dressed like that they swarmed her. Not us...her. I just happened to be next to her." She giggled before continuing. "I almost got impaled by a pen being shoved at her." Meredith turned her shoulder out to show where a long streak of ink marked the back side of her arm from a random autograph seeker. "I could never live like this."

"Whoa." Abi turned to Dani after seeing the ink mark battle scar on Meredith. "How do you stand it Dani?"

Dani stopped bouncing for a minute and appeared to consider the question before she finally shrugged it off. "What choice do I have? It's how I earn a living."

Abi noted that Dani's voice was flat and resisted the urge to say she felt sorry for her. It was a choice after all. Not one she would make, but evidently it was a compromise that Dani was willing to live with.

"I get that, but still…a girl's got to get a break sometime."

Dani laughed out loud. "That's a nice idea Abi, just not really my reality."

Abi turned toward the baggage carousel as Dani's frown just might make her sad to keep watching. She focused on the wheel turning. When the cycle was complete, she concentrated a little harder watching it go around again. She had not seen her bag in the mix. Her inner voice started the alarm that she could not quite voice yet. She had one change of clothes and a spare toothbrush in the bag she had carried on and it was nowhere near good enough for their night out tomorrow night. She reminded herself not to panic and gave herself a stern inner command, Whatever you do, do not start to cry.

Meredith moved to her side as she watched the bags continue to turn round. "What does yours look like, I'll help you grab it."

"Thanks. I don't see it." Abi responded desolately.

"You sure they said seven?"

Abi shrugged. "I thought so, just a minute."

She went to the board and double checked for her flight. Carousel seven was assigned to her arrival. The bag should be here. She had been to the airport and checked her bag, plus gotten a coffee and a spot at the charging counter at her gate a full two hours before departure. There was no last minute run that would account for it missing the flight.

"Yes, it says seven." She muttered as she returned.

"Okay, we'll give it a little bit before we go find someone. Maybe there's another cart to unload. It looks like a few other people are still waiting too." She smiled as she nodded down the row between the carousels.

"I hope you're right. That, or we'll have to go shopping. There's no way I'm wearing this out tomorrow night."

Meredith's smile grew. "Oh, we're going shopping anyway. There's a great outlet mall at Stateline. We decided while we were waiting. Hope you brought money to spend and not just to lose gambling."

"Oh I never gamble."

"Never?"

"Nope. Never."

Meredith's jaw dropped. "Really...never?"

Abi snorted. "No. Never, not once. For my luck it'd be simpler to toss it down the toilet. At least that way I don't get my hopes up."

Meredith laughed and sat on the edge of the carousel while they waited. Abi stood watching the crowd. Another throng had encircled Dani at the far end. Craning to see, Abi could not tell if Margo was in the midst of the crowd this time. She thought it would be funny if she were after her earlier assessment of Meredith being swallowed up. She kept that to herself.

Hearing another bag drop, she turned back to see if hers was coming, catching Margo sitting in a chair off to the side as she did. It was only after she turned fully that she absently noticed and had to turn back to confirm what she thought she had seen. Margo was sitting with her leg propped up. Her foot, ankle, and lower leg were all firmly encased in a stabilization boot. That can't be good. She thought as she watched more bags fall.

Thirteen bags later, Abi's brown suitcase finally came down the chute. She nearly sank with relief. She had brought spending money, but not so much as to invest into a new wardrobe for Vegas clubbing.

"That's me." She said pointing to the piece as it approached them.

Meredith jumped up and snatched it before Abi could, surprising her with the ease that she hefted the awkward bag.

"Whoa, you got some muscles hiding in your pocket." Abi snickered.

Meredith grinned wide. "Don't let my size fool you. I'm a tough-nut with strength to spare. Really, how many of us are actually what we seem?"

Abi wished she had a glass to raise but lifted her cupped hand in mock toast anyway. "Preach it sister!"

Meredith's smile faltered slightly. "Not gospel I'm sure, but the truth as I know it. Now let's get out of here."

"Deal!"

They moved together to the end area, head canting Margo to head over as they went to rescue Dani. Meredith shoved her way into the near inner circle of autograph hounds before raising her voice loudly.

"Danica is now off the clock folks. We have an appointment. Catch her next time."

Dani's face seemed a mix of relief and astonishment as the crowd moved off grumbling when Meredith seized her by her upper arm and pulled her from the crush of bodies. It was only after they were clear that Meredith's tone changed from all business to mocked ribbing.

"Lead the way Jeeves, where'd you park the car?"

The Custos Series
Book of Time

One book could change the world…or destroy it.

Ashmael Nocte and his mysterious group known only as the Custos are charged with protecting the book and its appointed Keeper. The equally secretive White Diamond society is determined to gain possession of the book, no matter what the cost.

The stakes are high as alliances are forged and broken, power and passion collide, and the world descends on New Orleans to celebrate the Mardi Gras of 1950.

This exciting prequel to Book of Change sets the stage with grudges as old as time, dangerous new desires, and a darkness that will haunt the Keeper and those who have vowed to keep her safe.

Available on eBook at amazon, and in print at fine booksellers everywhere: www.amzn.com/B01JJ5CL1W

BOOK OF TIME EXCERPT

TIME IS COMING

Ashmael Nocte looked like a man with the worry of the world set squarely on his shoulders. As the leader of the Custos, in many ways, he was just that. Dark and foreboding, his expression never changed from the deep furrow of his brows, to the firm set line of his lips. Even those of his troupe who knew him best, stepped aside to see him coming. He was not a male to tangle with.

He, and he alone, knew the lengths his nemesis would reach to force the pendulum to swing away from his control. Balance was always the goal, but never the status. It was always to one side or the other with the next shift teetering from a ledge, waiting for an unseen distant breeze to tip it again. Moments of calm were suspect. The twisted game had played out more times than he could count, and he was weary.

Ashmael strode into 43 Chartres like he owned the place, mostly because he did. It mattered little to him that it was on the even side of the street or in the 500 block. He had been in this place since before the Quarter, before the square, before the cathedral, and before those who called this plot of land in the deep basin 'home,' had known it existed.

Eternity was a laughable way to describe his existence. He is, he was, and he would always be. It was decreed before there was anything, and would continue long after the known world was scattered to the far reaches again.

Those who claimed the title of Custos would all one day claim their due rest, but not Ashmael. He would never know the touch or comfort of another, nor ever experience the ease that comes with laying down his burdens. His job, like that of the one he opposed, would never be complete.

From the outside looking in, number 43 was just another door in the wall, nothing impressive or noteworthy to the passersby who flocked to this stretch of pavement by the thousands day after day. From the inside, the creature comforts were plentiful. If one had to live forever, there had to be an up. Anything and everything he could want was available, except for a partner to share his load. Most days he didn't notice. Today was not that day.

It was nearly time for the book to change hands again. His nerves were zinging with overloading static from the heightened awareness and energy of the event. He'd give a great deal to be able to offload the excess. With any luck, this change would go as smoothly as the last one had thirty years before. Each Keeper was only tasked to do so for that length of time. To Ashmael, it seemed like it had been yesterday.

His deep set, dark eyes darted around the room at the others who were actively not looking back at him. Every Custos knew that one day their turn would come. Each was doing their best to remain grounded for the upcoming moment when they might be called to serve. It was never announced who would be the guardian for the new Keeper, they just were, and Ashmael didn't know who would be the one any more than they did. The guardians would all be in place for the exchange and one would just know. Like a key connecting into a tumbler, there was only one who would fit.

The bell over the door chimed as it opened and all heads turned to see who entered. Ashmael quirked a single brow high to see a female figure. It was not unheard of for a female Custos to be sent to serve, only uncommon. Then again, on occasion a tourist wandered in. His lip twitched with recognition of the newest body in the room as the back lit figure emerged from the halo cast by the closing door. This was no tourist.

"Weiss. It's been a long time." His quiet acknowledgement echoed through the room as he tipped the bottle of smoky bourbon to fill a glass on the counter.

"Nocte." She replied with a nod before taking in the others around the perimeter.

"Sassy britches!" came a challenging laugh from a shadowed corner before her eyes could penetrate it. "Must be a scramble coming this time if you've left the Farther Fields to join us for another round finally."

Weiss's hand came up to her chest and her head tossed back in mockery at the verbal jab. "You wound me Ardon West. I guess the creator knew you'd need help again huh? Sending a female to watch your back and all."

Ardon strode from his spot in the long shadow, his face set firmly in a scowl. "As if. You and I both know why you're here, and it isn't to watch me." He tapped his chin and held up a finger pointing to her nose. "Though, perhaps you should. Maybe you could learn a thing or two." He measured her up and down with slow deliberation and walked an arc around where she stood.

Weiss snorted loudly, stepped around Ardon to the counter opposite Ashmael, and nodded to the bottle. "I'll have one of those if you're pouring."

Ashmael pulled another glass from under the bar, setting it, and the bottle, side by side before turning to walk to the doorway at the end that lead to his private space. "Serve yourself." He called back as he disappeared.

If Weiss had facial hair, she would be stroking it. Instead, she looked like she was wiping crumbs from her mouth. Pouring a drink, she turned to the room once Ashmael closed the door he had passed through. "So it's gonna be like that?" she asked the room, but no one in particular.

"No, it ain't gonna be like that." A lean, lanky male replied coming forward. A pair of stormy hazel eyes found her before the words permeated. "White Diamond is everywhere lately. We're all on edge."

Weiss let a heavy sigh fall before she tipped the glass and

poured its contents down her throat in a single dump. "Tell me something I don't already know Greyson." She said setting the glass down. "I could walk on their backs from here to Canal and never touch the ground. I can't recall them ever being so obvious."

"They are getting desperate." He shrugged off. "The Keeper has managed to stay unfound the entire duration this time. That hasn't happened in ages. If they miss the exchange, they may have another thirty years to wait for a chance at the book." Greyson commented back quietly the fact that everyone else knew, but no one was saying.

Weiss's eyes shot wide. "She hasn't been found even once in thirty years?! Damn. Good for her." She nodded firmly. "Who's watching her?"

"Jensen." Greyson replied.

"Has he checked in?"

"No." Ardon interjected into the exchange firmly.

"So, we don't know if they are in town or close?" Weiss queried as she turned sharply, taking in the weight of the potential.

Everyone around the room shook their heads negatively in unison as though pulled by a common thread. Only Ardon spoke. "If Ashmael knows, he's the only one."

"Damn it." Weiss said under her breath before grating her lower teeth against her upper lip. "Anyone got any good news?"

She hadn't noticed the figure sitting near the vacant fireplace in the corner with their back to her, until Rourke stood, straightened his spine, and turned to face her. "We have a name."

Weiss slumped a little. It had been forever, if not forever plus a day since she'd seen Rourke. She gave herself a mental rebuke at the internal drama of her thoughts. Forty years was not forever, but they had trained together, watched out for one another, and lost track of each other when the Farther

Fields called her back thanks to a White Diamond she encountered. Forty years was forever enough in her mind.

She had never known if Rourke had fallen too, or managed to evade a killing blow. They were close as siblings with no blood between them. It was all she could do not to run to him, thankful he was here. She stared him down waiting for more, she nearly jumped when he didn't speak again for a long moment, and actually jumped when he finally did.

"When Rex makes his parade, the vine will bloom, and a rose will need to grow thorns." He said unblinkingly.

Rourke was still absorbing the shock of seeing Weiss standing inside 43 as he recited the passage. He had watched her fall in the skirmish so long ago, but could not stop then to know more. When she hadn't checked in again afterward, he had mourned at length the loss of his closest friend. She had put herself before him and paid the price in his place. He had cursed her for it ever since.

When she walked in, and he heard Ashmael acknowledge her, he had needed to remain facing the wall to get himself under control to see her. Would she be the same? He fought himself to be able to stand, turn, and finally check. Looking at her now, it was as though nothing had happened. She was still a compact powerhouse. Her musculature was evident under her clothes, and her eyes shown just as bright a blue as he remembered them to be. He wanted to shake her, he wanted to curse her, and he wanted to hug her. The conundrum and conflict was hard to bury beneath the stony face he normally wore.

When they realized simultaneously that no one else had spoken, they both tripped over their tongues to speak and talked over one another. It was the moment of levity the room needed. Loud laughter rang out from the dozen bodies that filled the space. Ardon clapped her on the shoulder before moving away back to where he had been. "Good to have you back with us Sassy."

Weiss groaned and snarled as she rolled her eyes. "Don't. Call. Me. That."

"Sure. Sure." He countered, waving her off as he turned away. "Whatever you say."

Weiss looked between Rourke and Greyson. "So, somebody catch me up."

The bell over the door tinkled again as the shadow of two large bookends crowded through the narrow arch, paused, exchanged a glance, and simultaneously rushed for Weiss.

"You're back!" they exclaimed together as she was smashed between the two large males. Landon and Langston were cut from the same cloth and seldom seen apart. It was rumored they wined and dined the females on Bourbon together too on any given night. The others speculated just how far their cooperative efforts really went, though no one knew for sure.

The ages melted away as they pulled back and set her down. Even now, after so many years, there was no doubt who was whom. Landon was an eyesore in his bright floral print shirt, and Langston was in a one pocket short-sleeve that likely had a few extra holes in it besides the ones for his arms and head. Their tastes in clothing could hardly be more different, but everything else was the same. Short, spikey, white blonde hair and fiercely dark chocolate eyes stared out from deeply tanned faces on both sides of her as she caught her breath. "Yes, I'm back. I could hardly let you guys have all the fun, now could I?"

The twins exchanged a mocking look, and like so many other things they did together, came back with the same reply. "Fun? We're having fun? Is that what we're calling it now?"

Weiss swatted them on opposite shoulders and shook her head. As though nothing had changed, the antics began.

It was good to be home. Langston grabbed her up in a giant bear hug as she laughed. "So much has happened while you were away sassy girl. The world has changed."

Weiss allowed herself to be led off by the two males, noting the others in the room who hadn't spoken as she passed them. There were a number of familiar faces, and a few she didn't know. She didn't have the heart to retort her thoughts to Langston that the world was always changing, and would continue to do so. For the encounter that was coming, a few moments of irresponsible glee would not hurt.

She hadn't been present for the last exchange, and would need to catch up soon. The one before it had been disastrous and she remembered it well, even though it had been successful. They had nearly lost the Keeper as the book reached their hands. Yes, the world had changed, but some things would forever be the same.

They were The Custos. The sacred guardians over every Child of Light, the Keepers of the book that held the world between its pages. They could not fail, or the world as it was known, would fall forever.

www.eclecticbardbooks.com

Made in the USA
Lexington, KY
18 August 2018